THE DRAGON'S PURSUIT

Lochguard Highland Dragons #7

JESSIE DONOVAN

Mythical Lake Press, LLC

The Dragon's Pursuit
Copyright © 2020 Laura Hoak-Kagey
Mythical Lake Press, LLC
First Print Edition

Cover Art by Clarissa Yeo of Yocla Designs
ISBN: 978-1944776022

The Stonefire and Lochguard series intertwine with one another. Since so many readers ask for the overall reading order, I've included it with this book. (This list is as of January 2020.)

Sacrificed to the Dragon (Stonefire Dragons #1)
Seducing the Dragon (Stonefire Dragons #2)
Revealing the Dragons (Stonefire Dragons #3)
Healed by the Dragon (Stonefire Dragons #4)
Reawakening the Dragon (Stonefire Dragons #5)
The Dragon's Dilemma (Lochguard Highland Dragons #1)
Loved by the Dragon (Stonefire Dragons #6)
The Dragon Guardian (Lochguard Highland Dragons #2)
Surrendering to the Dragon (Stonefire Dragons #7)
The Dragon's Heart (Lochguard Highland Dragons #3)
Cured by the Dragon (Stonefire Dragons #8)
The Dragon Warrior (Lochguard Highland Dragons #4)
Aiding the Dragon (Stonefire Dragons #9)
Finding the Dragon (Stonefire Dragons #10)
Craved by the Dragon (Stonefire Dragons #11)
The Dragon Family (Lochguard Highland Dragons #5)
Winning Skyhunter (Stonefire Dragons Universe #1)
The Dragon's Discovery (Lochguard Highland Dragons #6)
Transforming Snowridge (Stonefire Dragons Universe #2)
The Dragon's Pursuit (Lochguard Highland Dragons #7)
Persuading the Dragon (Stonefire Dragons #12 / May 14, 2020)

Short stories that can be enjoyed any time after the first few books:

Chapter One

D r. Layla MacFie did her best to focus on the mountain of paperwork on her desk as she waited for midnight to arrive.

Not because she liked to work late, but rather tonight was the night Chase McFarland would stop by to help set up some secret security cameras.

Her dragon spoke up. *I say use the time to change clothes and fix our hair.*

You might want to draw Chase's eye and entice him to kiss us, but not me. The lab coat, shirt, and trousers are fine.

Her inner beast huffed. *You may try to fool everyone else, but you can't fool me. We share the same dreams. Like this one.*

Her dragon flashed images inside their brain of Chase pinning their hands above their head as he thrust deep inside her, making her moan as their bodies gleamed lightly with sweat, each of them crying out as they orgasmed at the same time.

Layla tossed aside her pen and growled. *Stop it. Chase*

is doing us a favor, nothing more. And no matter how many times you try to change my mind about resisting him, it won't work.

Which makes you an idiot, and that's saying something since you can be brilliant most of the time.

Her brows furrowed as she debated tossing her dragon inside a mental prison. Part of her dragon's behavior was Layla's fault. After all, dragons needed sex on a semi-regular basis, and it had been years since Layla had slept with any male. Mostly because of the sudden onslaught of responsibilities when she'd been promoted to Lochguard's head doctor, and she'd simply been too tired to smile or try to charm some male into bed.

But her dragon wasn't completely innocent, either. The bloody beast seemed focused on a male they shouldn't have. Not just because he was so much younger than them, which usually meant he'd be more likely to flee when things turned difficult, but also because Layla had to find her partners outside the clan, if possible. As the clan's head doctor, she needed to keep close yet distant relations with everyone. That made it easier if she had to cut them open for surgery, or if she needed to make split-second decisions when faced with a life or death situation.

Her dragon chimed in again. *Maybe there's a reason Chase has fancied us for so long. If he's our true mate, then is that something you want to pass up?*

She blinked. *It's almost unheard of for an older female to be the true mate of a much younger male. You know the instinct exists for one thing—to keep the species alive. Even if I were open to having a child—which my schedule most certainly doesn't allow—there is a much greater risk because of my age.*

We're thirty-five, not fifty. It's young enough.

She rubbed her forehead. *Did you miss the point where I said I don't want a child? There's no other doctor experienced enough to take care of Lochguard in my absence. And there would need to be someone here to help for any pregnancy I had, not to mention the ensuing recovery.*

Gregor would come back to help us if we asked.

Gregor Innes had previously been Lochguard's head doctor. Then he'd found his true mate in a dragon-shifter doctor from Clan Stonefire, in the South of England, and now lived there with his mate and newborn son. Layla had been—and still was—happy for her former boss. But him leaving had also left her extremely short-handed, especially with all the pregnant mates and new bairns born in the last year or two.

She replied to her beast, *No, we can't ask him to come back. Gregor has enough to worry about, and taking a male away from his family for any period of time would be a disaster. And that's not a risk I'm willing to take.*

So instead, you'd rather just be alone, isolated, and live life as a robot?

Now, wait a minute, dragon, that's unfair. You try to deny it, but we both love helping others. A robot wouldn't care one way or the other.

Before her beast could respond, a familiar male voice filled her office. "You're frowning quite hard, lass. And since I'm a few minutes early, it can't be about me."

Layla lifted her head and met Chase's dark brown gaze.

The slight upturn of his lips and the intensity of his

stare sent a rush of heat through her body, as well as a wee bit of longing.

What she wouldn't give to have a partner in all ways, one whom she could share everything with. She loved her dragon, but the inner half was part of her and couldn't help her with most things. It wasn't the same as a mate.

No. Layla couldn't take a mate. It was her duty to take care of the clan.

Clearing her throat, she stood. Careful to keep the desk between them, she said, "I'm worried about the ever-growing list of stolen medical supplies, that's all."

He raised a light brown eyebrow, which was several shades darker than his blond hair. "You've never been a good liar, Layla."

Silently cursing her inability to deceive, she stood taller. "Not all of us were hooligans in our youth, Chase."

He grinned unabashedly. Layla tried her best to ignore his dimples as he said, "It was more fun that way. The old clan leader was quite strict, aye? And while my mum and brother were too good to annoy him, someone had to."

She snorted. "You were just trying to imitate Finn."

Finn Stewart was Lochguard's current clan leader and one of Layla's greatest allies. However, he'd been quite the troublemaker when he'd been younger. He still could be, but his mate and clan responsibilities had tamed him down considerably.

Chase shrugged. "No one could match his penchant for trouble, but I like to think I came close. Not to mention, I got to see more humans than most during my secret trips to Inverness, and that required its own sort of skill, to sneak out unnoticed."

Shaking her head, she leaned against her desk a fraction. "I wouldn't call them secret, let alone unnoticed. Your poor mother had to send out a search party once, when you gave no notice and didn't return in the morning."

His expression instantly turned solemn. "I do regret that, aye."

Layla had always had an instinct that allowed her to sense when people were holding back information. It was one of the many reasons she was a good dragon-shifter doctor.

And her internal alarm was ringing quite loudly inside her head.

Her beast spoke up. *Don't bring up his mother and her bastard ex-mate. That would ruin any chance we have of getting him naked.*

Chase's mother had barely been able to leave her cottage when her mate abandoned her a couple years ago. No matter what they'd tried, she'd kept to herself. Both Layla and her former boss had suspected Gillian might die of heartbreak. However, Gillian McFarland had somehow managed to weather being abandoned by the male she loved, probably in large part due to her two sons spending time with her whenever they could.

Given how her sons were the reason she'd probably stayed on Lochguard when Finn had given his ultimatum —accept his leadership position and decision to build relationships with humans or fend for themselves—it made sense that they'd been able to bring her back to the land of the living bit by bit.

And if Layla were a petty person, she'd bring up Chase's mother to dour the mood. But Layla wasn't that kind of person. Her entire life centered on making people whole and happy. She couldn't change that if she tried.

So she focused on the favor she needed from Chase. Making her way around the desk, careful to keep some distance between her and the male, she moved to the door. "Come, you must be tired after a full day's work of wiring the new warehouse. The sooner I show you where I want the cameras, the better."

Humor danced in his eyes. "So you know my schedule? Interesting. Do you keep track of everyone inside the clan then? If so, maybe you could give my brother some pointers or feed him the intel. Ever since his mate became pregnant, he's become mostly useless."

Layla snorted. "I dare you to tell that to his face."

He winked, and damn it, like every time before, the action made Layla's stomach flutter.

He stated proudly, "I have many, many times."

Since Chase's older brother was a co-head Protector for Lochguard, in charge of clan security, she could just imagine the quiet, growly male putting up with his brother's teasing. "You know, I always wanted a younger brother growing up, but now I'm not so sure. You lot tend to make your older siblings' life miserable."

He grinned. "I like to think it's more of me relaxing Grant a bit. All the responsibility he has takes its toll. And while many people are afraid or cower a bit before him, he's just my brother." He tilted his head a fraction. "I'm sure your sister teased you the same way, aye?"

People rarely talked about Layla's younger sister. Yasmin had succumbed to her parents' pressure for an arranged mating with a dragonman in Iran, where her mother's family had originally come from. No one had heard from her in years.

Not wanting to think of Yasmin and how much Layla missed her sister, she changed the subject. "Come on, it's late. Let's go before someone bursts through the front doors with an emergency."

She walked past Chase, careful not to touch him. Not touching him would be the easy part, though. For some reason, he made her want to talk about things she never talked about, like about her younger sister. And she couldn't acknowledge how nice it was to be merely a dragonwoman and not a doctor, a female with her own family, past, and troubles.

Her dragon growled. *You spend all your time making others happy, but we deserve it, too. Chase could be the future we need.*

Not in the mood to argue yet again with her beast, she quickly tossed her dragon inside a mental prison.

Layla had decided her life's path long ago, and she'd chosen medicine, end of story. Besides, once she made a decision, it was hard to change her mind. And why would she want to? She had the power to heal and help nearly as many people as the clan leader.

All she needed to do was survive a short while alone with Chase and then she could distract herself with work again.

So she walked faster toward her destination, not even

checking to see if Chase followed her or not. The sooner she finished this task, the sooner she could move on to the next one and, once again, push all thoughts of the male from her head.

As Chase McFarland followed Layla down the corridor, he couldn't help but stare at her arse. True, it was hidden underneath her lab coat, but Chase had her entire body and all of its curves memorized.

It was what any male would do with the true mate he may never have.

Dragon-shifters hit full maturity at twenty. And the day after his twentieth birthday, Chase had taken one look at Layla MacFie and had been hit with an all-consuming need and desire, wanting the one female above all others. He'd fought it at first, but soon acknowledged the inevitable—Layla was his true mate, the one fate thought to be his best chance at happiness.

Over the last two years, he'd somehow found the strength to resist kissing her and start a mate-claim frenzy that would only end with a pregnancy. And while some males would give in to their dragon's constant demands and face the consequences later, Chase would never be that person. That exact same situation had caused his aunt and uncle a lifetime of misery, and he would never do that to a female.

His dragon huffed. *We are not our uncle. Besides, recently Layla has been noticing us more and may not resist. Tell her the truth. I'm tired of waiting.*

Two years ago, Chase had tried to suggest to his inner beast about finding another female. His dragon had roared and nearly gone rogue at the idea. He wanted Layla, and only her.

And so that was how Chase had learned self-control and patience, which had matured him much faster than any of his friends or others his age.

He replied to his dragon, *No. I tried being charming, visiting her, and pursuing her like you wanted. That didn't work. Now we're doing it my way.*

His dragon huffed. *It means more waiting. And proving ourself to her may not be enough. She needs a wee bit of encouragement. Especially since she's stubborn, to the point she'll hold on to her chosen path, no matter the bloody consequences toward her own well-being.*

Sometimes, Chase hated how closely his dragon had paid attention to Layla over the years. It made it harder to win an argument about the lass.

But he wasn't giving up. *She needs our help right now. Even you can't deny her that, aye? So no more sex fantasies or blasts of lust. No matter what you may think, our cock can't install security cameras.*

It'd be fun to try. Maybe it'd even impress Layla. If we could do that, just imagine what we could do to her when she was naked.

He resisted a sigh. Everyone gave Chase a hard time about being a cheeky troublemaker, but they didn't know his dragon could be loads worse.

Thankfully Layla stopped in front of a door, and his beast curled into a ball with a grunt. He'd watch and probably fall asleep while Chase fulfilled their promise to Layla.

Honorable dragons always kept their promises, and not for the first time, Chase was happy as fuck that his beast was one of them, unlike his bastard father.

Careful to keep a smile on his face and not let his thoughts show, he stopped a little closer than was proper to Layla. Her breath hitched, but he managed to keep his cock in line as he asked, "In here then?"

For a second, Layla's beautiful dark brown eyes stared into his, her pupils flashing to slits and back to round once more. He'd never managed to have a conversation with her dragon, and not for the first time, he wondered if her beast was on Team Chase or not.

Layla cleared her throat and took a step back. His every instinct was to follow her, but he held his ground. Chase would stick to his plan to prove his worth as a future mate, no matter what. Layla may be stubborn and strong-willed, but so was he.

She whispered, "Aye, in here." Opening the door, she pointed to a spot on the wall inside the room. "Put it over there."

He stepped inside the large supply closet, took Layla's hand, and tugged her inside. She gently fell against his arm for a second, and he enjoyed the softness of her breast before she stood upright.

After shutting the door, she turned back toward him with a frown. "There's no need to tug me around. I can walk."

His lips twitched. Dragon-shifter doctors almost always threaded steel into their voices, and Layla was no exception. Too bad Chase was good at defying orders when he wanted. "And I'm the one doing you a favor, aye? So no need to reprimand me for something so minor."

"I wasn't reprimanding you." She tried to put distance between them, but only managed an inch. "A reprimand would be more like this." Layla schooled her face into a stern expression, her brows raised for emphasis. "Tugging people around can be dangerous and cause injury. I'd suggest not doing it again, to save me the future work."

While she was trying to be serious, all Chase wanted to do was lean over and kiss her lips until they changed from a firm line, to open and seeking beneath his.

Dragon, stop with the images.

I wasn't doing anything. It's all you.

He replied to the doctor, "Leading people around is probably about the least dangerous thing I do, lass. Are you sure you want to waste your reprimand on that?"

She growled again, the act softened by the way her hair fell over her shoulders. All he wanted to do was reach up and touch the softness. Her voice snapped him back to the present, though. "I know your reputation, Chase McFarland. And since I don't want to turn gray before I finish the list of everything you shouldn't do, I won't start going through it."

He tried not to wince. Reputations weren't always true, and a large chunk of his most certainly wasn't. He hoped Layla didn't think he'd bedded half the single human females of Inverness, as his friends suggested. True, he'd had to hint at something to keep everyone from learning about Layla being his true mate before she was ready. But it still mattered to him what Layla thought of his reputation.

His dragon chimed in. *Screw our reputation. The truth is we haven't had anyone for two years. Kiss her, now, and change that.*

No. He focused back on Layla. "You'd look bonnie with gray hair, lass. So start listing away."

"Stop calling me 'lass.' I'm too old for that."

He should hold back, but the words flew off Chase's tongue before he could stop it. "You're not old, Layla. You're perfect."

Her cheeks turned pink as she stared at him.

Damn, she was so bloody beautiful. Dark hair and eyes, all topped off with lovely olive skin inherited from her mother's side. It made him wonder if her nipples would be a little darker because of her delicious light brown complexion or not.

You could easily find out, his beast stated.

Layla's pupils turned slitted for a few beats. Her cheeks turned even redder. Maybe her dragon was on his side after all.

She finally spoke again, her voice echoing inside the small room. "Can you put the first camera there?"

She pointed to a spot just over his shoulder. Maybe some people would do a double take at the change of subject, but Layla did it as often as breathing.

It was her way of trying to create distance.

Reminded of his task to be reliable and show how he was a male she could trust, he turned away from her and took a step closer to the wall.

He'd studied the schematics of the surgery earlier,

and quickly imagined where all the electrical wires were hidden inside the walls. Taking out a pencil, he marked the area she'd indicated, so he could remember and confirm the placement was good. "Aye, it should be fine, and if not, I'll let you know once I take out my tools. Now, show me all the rest of the places you want cameras installed and then I'll get to work."

Layla reached around him and snatched the pencil from his hand. The light brush of her fingers against his made blood rush south. Thank fuck he was facing a wall and not Layla. She was bound to notice his erection in such close quarters.

His dragon hummed. *Turn and bump into her. Let her feel how we want her.*

Stop it, dragon. Now.

Layla stepped back and used her detached doctor's voice again. "I'll go and mark all the spots whilst you work here. That way, I can quickly show you the rooms and not get in your way."

He wished he could say she wouldn't get in the way. But even now, Layla's scent had taken over the storage closet, and it made it harder for him to concentrate by the minute.

Setting his bag of tools down, he nodded. "Aye, that will work. Give me half an hour to turn off the power to this room and install the first camera. Then come back and get me. Once they're all done, I can show you how to use them."

"Okay," she answered quickly before leaving the room.

The second Layla was gone, the room felt colder and emptier.

Pushing aside the ridiculous notion since it wasn't as if he could drag her back and kiss her senseless, Chase laid out what he needed for the job and went to shut off the breaker.

Chapter Two

L ayla was in the middle of a dream about racing her
younger sister along the northern coast of Scotland
when a male voice reached her. "Layla, lass, wake up."

She jumped upright, blinking to try and bring everything into focus.

Her dragon murmured, *It's just Chase.*

Sure enough, the male stood next to her desk, looking
as sexy as ever with his slightly tousled hair, as if he'd ran
his hands through it while thinking.

Get a grip, Layla. You've seen sexy males before. When she
noticed his twitching lips, it fully brought her back to the
present, and she barked, "What?"

"Someone doesn't wake up easily, aye?"

It was on the tip of her tongue to say she usually
jumped out of bed with a smile, but she hadn't slept in
nearly twenty-four hours and was groggy. However, a
doctor needed to appear invincible and alert to give the

clan confidence in her abilities. It was better he thought her slow to wake up than admit she was bone-weary.

Her dragon tilted her head a fraction inside her mind. *Why? His older brother works long hours sometimes, so Chase understands. He wouldn't think us weak.*

She didn't reply because Chase pointed to the side of her face, just below the corner of his mouth, and added, "You might want to wipe your chin before I show you how to use the cameras. We don't want any drool dripping onto the equipment, now, do we?"

With a grunt, Layla instantly wiped her face and then smoothed her hair. So much for appearing put-together. "Just show me how to operate them quickly so that we can both get some sleep."

His pupils flashed and held for a few beats before returning to round. Layla always wished she could hear other inner dragons. That would make her work easier, for one.

Chase leaned over and placed a hand on the desk. Even though he wasn't touching her, heat radiated from his body, and she nearly leaned into it.

His deep voice filled the room. "I need to install the last bits in here, so you can check the cameras. Unless you'd rather they transmit to your home?"

Being alone with Chase in her home would be a bad idea. The surgery gave Layla courage and a way to buffer herself from him and his addictive male scent.

And yet, Layla didn't know who she could trust in the surgery. She would need to check the footage from her home, which meant finding the strength to resist Chase.

Pushing her long black hair away from her face and

over her shoulder, she met his gaze without hesitation. Ignoring how the brown irises had flecks of gold around the pupil, she answered, "My home would be better. Although it's late, so maybe we should save it for another time?"

"Why? If you're as concerned as you say, then you'd want to start recording and watching out for the thief straight away, aye? As long as you can walk me to your cottage and let me in, I can do all the work whilst you nap again." He winked. "It's one of the benefits of being so young—I have lots of energy."

Her dragon grunted. *Exactly. Imagine all the energy focused on us. He might be able to even wear me out in bed.*

Stop it, dragon. Layla spoke aloud, "I routinely stay awake for twenty or thirty hours straight. It's more a matter of whether you can keep up with me."

She expected him to tease her, but his gaze turned serious as he said, "You work too much, lass. You need to take better care of yourself."

With most people in the clan, she'd brush off the comment. Apart from the clan leader and possibly the heads of security, Layla had absolute authority over everyone else. She wasn't used to people telling her what to do, let alone anyone noticing how she worked too much. Usually, they were more concerned about their latest injury or problem and wanted Layla to fix it.

Chase, on the other hand, seemed to notice too much.

She gently pushed against Chase's side until he stood up straight. She followed suit and rose to her feet. "If I work less, people can die or suffer unnecessarily. So unless you can provide another fully trained doctor out of thin air, you'll leave me alone to take care of the clan."

He stood close enough that she felt his breath on her cheek as he said, "There are others who could help you more, if you asked. Besides, you talked to that Seahaven doctor at the gathering not long ago. I thought he was going to start coming here sometimes?"

Clan Seahaven was a smaller splinter dragon clan that had once been part of Lochguard. Under a different leader, they'd fled with their human mates and established their own homes. It was only recently, under Finn's leadership, that the two clans had even started talking with one another.

And aye, their doctor had promised to visit once a week to help with patients and exchange information. But how the bloody hell Chase knew all that, she didn't know. It wasn't exactly public knowledge.

Chase reached out a hand as if to touch her jaw, but then curled his fingers into a fist and pulled back. He grunted. "I wish you'd talk to me, Layla. You shoulder so much and need someone at your side. Not because you're weak, but because you deserve to have someone to lean on and help take on responsibilities. Or, at the very least, be there to listen to a rant or help you relax after a rough day."

Her dragon spoke up. *He's right, you know. You may appear surrounded by clan all the time, but we're actually quite isolated. Chase could change all that and make life brighter. And most definitely help us relax. Many times a day, in fact. He may even let me mark his back with my talons.*

Careful not to encourage her beast when it came to

24

sex with Chase, she replied, *We can't afford the distraction, and you know it.*

Would it be a distraction, though? You always counsel others to speak their minds and the truth. Why are we different?

Because lives could be at stake.

Chase's voice prevented Layla from replying to her beast. "Sit down."

She blinked at the dominance in his voice. "What?"

"Sit down, lass. Just for a few moments."

The urge to obey his command coursed through her body, but she resisted. "We need to get to my cottage and finish the job."

"Sit."

She studied his face a second before saying, "You're not going to stop saying that, are you?"

He grinned. "Sit."

Rolling her eyes, Layla sat. "See? I'm sitting. How long do I need to be here? Sixty seconds? Ninety? Tell me so I can start counting."

"As long as it takes for me to help you relax."

Before she could do more than meet his gaze again, he moved behind her and placed his hands on her shoulders. Despite the layers of clothing, she felt the delicious heat of his fingers and couldn't hold back a gasp.

She expected him to tease her, but he remained silent as he massaged her shoulders, pressing his thumbs firmly into the knotted tension of her muscles.

Her dragon hummed as he continued to work, and Layla's head fell forward with each movement of Chase's fingers.

Layla eventually moaned as he reached a particularly tense area and Chase said, "Nearly there, lass."

So content, Layla took a second to recognize what he was talking about—giving up when she was finally relaxed.

Her dragon spoke up. *I could get used to this.*

Normally, she'd protest and give a list of reasons why they never could. However, as Chase's fingers pressed into her neck and shoulders, she couldn't think of why she couldn't have this every day.

And then Chase's touch was gone and she nearly whimpered. Layla couldn't remember the last time a male's touch had been so firm yet gentle, not to mention able to turn her brain to a nearly useless pile of jelly.

He moved to stand at her side again and offered his hand. "Come, Layla. I can carry you if you like, but I thought I'd ask first. You know, to prevent any possible injury that you'd have to take care of after the fact."

She smiled without thinking, amused at him throwing her words back at her. "How kind of you."

Chase winked, the action making her belly flip. The male was too handsome for his own good.

He murmured, "I wouldn't say I can be fully trained, but I'm always open to learning, lass. Especially when it concerns you."

THE SECOND THE words left Chase's lips, he knew he'd fucked up.

His entire plan had been to prove his worth to Layla

26

before hinting she was his true mate. And clever lass that she was, Layla may now know the truth. Or very soon would figure it out.

His dragon spoke up. *Good. She's extremely intelligent, and I hope she'll ask questions and figure it out. I'm tired of hiding it.*

Layla's question came out slowly. "Why me? There are both dragon-shifter females and human females who've all but thrown themselves at you. So why me especially?"

Maybe he was a bit of a bastard, but he liked that she'd noticed how some of the females had acted with him. Not that any of them compared to Layla.

Chase took a second to debate what to do before replying, "You're beautiful, smart, loyal, and kinder than almost anyone I've met. On top of that, you don't play games like the others. You speak your mind and know enough about the world to recognize life is short and always encourage everyone to embrace what joy they can find." He paused and added quietly, "Well, you encourage everyone except yourself for some reason."

His beast growled. *Which is why you need to tell her the full truth, and maybe she'll embrace it.*

Ignoring his dragon, he dared a step closer. Layla didn't retreat, and it encouraged him to add, "I suppose I should be asking you why not me? I want you, Layla MacFie, and I would take every free moment you had to convince you of it. Look past numbers on a page and truly look at me, lass. Why not me?"

Her pupils flashed as she studied his gaze. Damn, what he wouldn't give to know what her dragon was saying.

Probably that she agrees with us and wants us. Even if female dragons don't fully recognize a true mate pull until they're kissed, there's probably some sense of wanting on her end.

Chase should tell Layla the truth right here, right now. But as she bit her lower lip, he couldn't bring himself to do it. Oh, he'd absolutely tell her before he kissed the lass, but was it wrong to want Layla to desire him simply for himself instead of the instinct?

Because the instinct's pull would fade over time, like it had with his aunt, uncle, and a few other couples on Lochguard, and they could both end up miserable for the rest of their lives.

Layla's voice was barely a whisper as she replied, "I work all the time."

"Not all the time. And when you're off, I'll be there waiting for you."

"I don't do flings, which is all you'll want."

"No, I want you, Layla. End of story."

"But you don't even know me," she whispered.

He dared to brush a stray strand of hair behind her ear, allowing his finger to linger against her skin. Layla drew in a breath and it sent heat rushing through his body. His voice was husky as he said, "Then give me the chance to do so, lass. Because I want to. I really do."

His heart raced as she continued to stare into his eyes. He wanted nothing more than to pull her head close, kiss her jaw, and murmur further words of encouragement.

However, he sensed Layla needed to sort through her thoughts in this moment, right here, before he could do anything else. If she still resisted him after all he'd said this evening, he may never have a chance with her.

Not because he didn't want her, but because she might be too guarded to ever allow him in.

He barely heard her reply. "I'm afraid if I do, it might break me in the end."

With a growl, he took her face in his hands and lightly stroked her skin. "I would never hurt you, Layla. Once I set my mind on something, I stick to it, even if the world thinks I'm nothing but a charming, happy-go-lucky bloke who doesn't have a care in the world. And if you say yes, if you choose me, then I would be the most dedicated male ever."

She opened her mouth to ask a question, but a knock on the door made her jump.

Chase quickly dropped his hands and stepped away from the lass. Image was everything for a clan doctor, and if he wanted any chance with her, he needed to prove he respected that. In other words, he'd have to wait for her to touch him in front of others and not the other way around.

His dragon grumbled, *I want to hurt whoever is on the other side of the door for interrupting. She might've been about to say yes and finally given us a chance.*

Hush, dragon. Not now.

Layla stated for the person to enter, and the tall, blond form of one of Lochguard's nurses—Logan Lamont—appeared in the doorway. "Here you are. It's Aimee King. She's having an episode again, and Arabella needs your help. They're both at the cottage next to Finn and Ara's place."

Layla's entire body went on alert. "I'll be right there. Gather the usual supplies, and I'll meet you at the cottage."

With a nod, Logan closed the door. Layla quickly opened a drawer, picked up a set of keys, and handed them to him. "Install what you need to in my place. I need to help Aimee."

He took the keys and did his best to hide any disappointment. "Aye, I'll do that. And whilst I'll get it all sorted, I'll find you later to explain how they work."

With a curt nod, Layla hurried to her doctor's bag, picked it up, and left the room.

Chase curled his fingers over the keys. He was fairly certain he'd convinced Layla that he was worth noticing. The trick would be to ensure she didn't try to pretend this evening had never happened.

His dragon huffed. *Aye, well, we'll find her tomorrow and remind her, which means we'll have to corner Layla in her home. Once we're alone, we can try again.*

Aye, you're right. Tomorrow can't come soon enough.

Exiting the office, Chase gathered his remaining tools and left the surgery. At least he'd have some time in Layla's home. Not that he'd go snooping around, but her scent would be everywhere, which should help calm both man and beast for a wee while until they could see her again.

Chapter Three

As Layla half ran toward Aimee King's temporary cottage, she slowly packed away the moment she'd just had with Chase.

Every word about her, and his wanting her, had rung with truth. And he acted far more mature than any twenty-two-year-old should.

Her dragon spoke up. *His father abandoned him a couple of years ago, and he's had to help his mother with her grief. That would do it.*

Maybe. But I sense he's holding something back, something important.

But before she could replay her conversation with the male in question, she reached the correct cottage and knocked on the door. It instantly opened to reveal Holly MacKenzie, one of the human females mated to a Lochguard dragonman. And more importantly, Holly was one of Layla's part-time nurses.

Holly rushed her inside. "It's worse this time, Layla. I think she's reliving some of the worst of her torture."

Layla ignored the constricting of her heart. Aimee King was from Clan Skyhunter, in the South of England. While her brother was now one of the co-leaders of the clan, the old ruler had gone to extreme measures to keep his power for as long as he could manage it. As a result, Aimee had been one of many who'd been tossed into prison, their dragons silenced and then tortured if they didn't plead their loyalty. While many of the older clan members had survived and were slowly moving on, Aimee had only been eighteen at the time, not even fully mature by dragon standards.

As a result, Aimee's trauma had been more severe.

Layla replied to Holly, "Giving her a light, mostly dragon-friendly sedative is risky. We'll have to try and force the herbal tea down her throat to calm her down and allow her to sleep."

Layla had worked with the doctors on Stonefire to develop the tea. Something similar had been given to Arabella when she'd been younger and had been dealing with her own PTSD from being set on fire by dragon hunters in her teenage years.

Holly bobbed her head. "I have the hot water ready and waiting. Give the order, and I'll ensure she takes it myself."

"No, Logan should be the one to do it. Dragon-shifters are stronger than humans, as much as I'm sure you didn't wish it sometimes. Besides, we can't have the mother of the two future peacemakers of our kind hurt by a random punch or kick."

Holly rolled her eyes. "Not you, too. The twins will be wee troublemakers given their father, aye. But nothing more."

Holly had twin females, which was extremely rare amongst dragon-shifters. Even though Layla didn't quite believe in the legends of how twin females brought periodic peace to their kind, teasing the human mother often helped with stress and tension. And keeping her staff somewhat relaxed was one of the many aspects of Layla's job.

The sound of growls and something hitting the wall grew louder as they reached the doorway of one of the bedrooms.

Inside, a dark-haired female stood in a corner, growling and banging against the walls with her palms.

It was Aimee.

About five feet away from the troubled lass stood Arabella, the mate of Lochguard's clan leader and the main person in charge of taking care of Aimee.

Layla slowed her pace as she entered the room, careful to keep her distance from the unstable female. Layla whispered to Arabella, "Has anything worked to help calm her down?"

Arabella kept her eyes fixed on Aimee as she answered, "The video of my daughter in dragon form helped at first, her little squeaky roars stopping Aimee from shredding the bed with her nails. But as soon as the video ended, Aimee jumped into the corner, started her current actions, and nothing has worked to calm her down."

Layla bobbed her head. All inner dragons acted on

instinct, and even in her dragon's silent form, the need to calm down for a young must've coursed through Aimee, which was why the video had been used before.

A real child's presence might be even more effective. However, Layla wasn't about to bring any child close to Aimee in her current state, no matter how calming it might be.

She said to Holly, "Find Logan so we can give her the tea."

Trusting the human to carry out her order, Layla focused all of her attention on Aimee. She waited for the younger female to meet her gaze. Once she did, Layla threaded dominance into her voice while still being gentle. "Aimee, I know you can hear me, aye? My accent alone tells you I'm not from Skyhunter. None of the males who hurt you are here, nor will they be able to get to you."

It didn't always work, but Aimee tended to respond more positively to dominant females than males. In a few beats, Aimee looked away as her hands dropped to her side, finally still.

Layla chanced a step forward, but the other female growled, so she stayed put. "Everyone here only wants to help you, lass. Can you tell us what happened? If there's anything in my power to do, I'll do it to help you, Aimee. But you need to talk with us first."

The female kept her gaze on the floor, and Layla waited patiently.

Aimee had only started talking in bits and pieces over the last few weeks. A huge improvement over her previous state, when she hadn't said a word, but it still wasn't enough for Layla or Arabella to really discover the root cause of all her terrors and nightmares. Bad dreams or PTSD were one thing. But if it were her dragon flashing horrifying thoughts and visions, that was another.

No. Layla wouldn't think of that outcome just yet because it could mean silencing Aimee's dragon for good to prevent her from turning rogue.

And Layla would do anything to prevent Aimee's dragon from going rogue. Those who couldn't control their inner beasts were usually hunted down and killed by the human government.

She felt her dragon stir in her mind but remained quiet. Her inner beast knew better than to make Layla's pupils change and send Aimee into yet another hysterical state—they'd all learned that lesson early on.

After a full minute, Layla asked gently, "Was it a nightmare?"

Aimee shook her head only a fraction, but it was enough. So Layla continued, "Bad memories?"

Aimee's fingers curled into fists, and she nodded as a tear rolled down her cheek.

Layla wanted nothing more than to go over and hug the lass, but she held back. Touching Aimee would only make things worse.

So instead, she continued speaking gently, needing to ask at least one more question even if it would cause the lass a wee bit of distress. "And did your dragon talk to you or try to make you feel even worse?"

Aimee tensed in the corner of the room, and Layla held her breath. The next minute or so would tell her if

Aimee was indeed improving or not. Because if she went silent, curled up into a ball, and shut everyone out again, then the lass wouldn't be much better than when she'd first arrived.

While it was Layla's job to do no harm, that little provision might be temporarily forgotten if she ever came face-to-face with the bastards who'd hurt Aimee King.

Finally, Aimee spoke, her voice no more than a murmur, "No, no dragon. She's still silent."

Layla inwardly let out a sigh of relief. She had at least another day of thinking positive thoughts concerning Aimee's future.

She replied, "Thank you, Aimee." From the corner of her eye, Layla noticed Logan in the doorway holding a mug. She continued, "You remember Logan, aye? He's brought a special tea for you, one that helps you sleep without nightmares." Aimee's eyes widened, but Layla hurriedly said, "The tea won't harm you. I promise. Watch."

Layla crossed the floor to the door, took the mug from Logan, and went back to the spot where she'd been standing. She quickly took a drink of the hot, bitter tea. "See? It'll only help you relax. Nothing more."

Aimee's gaze darted to Logan and away. The lass had trouble with most males and had learned to tolerate Logan if necessary. However, she would grow even more reserved if he entered.

Sort of a catch-22 since Layla sometimes needed a male dragon-shifter's strength to keep Aimee from hurting herself.

Focusing solely on the troubled lass, Layla offered the mug. "If you drink it yourself, then Logan can stay over there. He'll only come in if you resist."

One second passed, and then another. Finally, Aimee rushed over, took the mug, and went back to her corner.

She quietly drank the tea, and Layla motioned Logan and Holly away from the door, and they closed it after themselves. Once it was only her and Arabella with the lass, Layla spoke again. "You'll feel sleepy soon enough. Do you want me or Ara to help you to bed?"

Aimee didn't hesitate. "Ara."

"Aye, then I'll leave you two alone." She went to the door but paused before opening it. "Unless there's anything else you want to tell me, Aimee?"

Every time Layla asked the question, she hoped for an answer.

However, Aimee shook her head and finished off her tea. Taking her cue, Layla left the two females alone and went toward the kitchen.

Her dragon finally spoke up. *She's not worse. That's something.*

I know. I just wish she'd see the psychologist.

Dragon-shifter psychologists were even rarer than doctors. There were only two in the entire UK, and neither were from Lochguard.

And for whatever reason, Aimee had only warmed up to dragon-shifters who lived on Lochguard.

Her dragon replied, *We and Ara are doing our best. And Aimee is better. Take joy in the progress she's made so far and accept that not even you can perform miracles, no matter how hard you try to make them happen.*

37

Layla grunted but didn't reply as she entered the kitchen. Holly and Logan had cleaned up the room, as well as refreshed the necessary medical supplies needed for almost any emergency with Aimee.

Holly was the first to speak. "You calmed her down, which is a relief. I hate having to force her to do anything."

Logan offered Layla a cup of black tea, and she gratefully took it. After a sip of the hot, slightly bitter liquid, she replied, "All we can do is take it one day at a time. Although if she keeps talking and revealing more bit by bit, it may give me more clues in how to treat her."

Holly asked, "Have Sid and Gregor found out anything from the other doctors?"

Sid and Gregor, Stonefire's main doctors and a mated pair, were trying to create a worldwide sharing and networking database for dragon-shifter doctors. Layla often asked about their progress, hoping to use some of their methods to one day reach out to human doctors as well. "No, not yet. But they'll keep trying. Don't worry."

They chatted a bit about clan news until Arabella appeared in the kitchen. Without preamble, she said, "I want Aimee to meet Freya."

Freya was Arabella's wee daughter. Layla blinked. "What?"

Arabella shrugged. "It's not such a strange suggestion. After all, the video works well with Aimee, and I think the real thing might help her even more. With Freya around, she might even start talking more. We won't know until we try."

Freya wasn't even a year old and had started shifting

38

into a dragon much earlier than usual. As a result, she was the darling of the entire clan, but none more so than to her father. Layla replied, "Finn will never allow it, aye? And I'm not about to suggest it to him."

Arabella waved a hand in dismissal. "I'll convince him to do it, even if it takes a day or two. He knows I'd never intentionally put Freya in harm's way. And his entire job is to help the clan, just like you, Layla, albeit in different ways. Even if Aimee is merely a foster, that doesn't matter to Finn. Anyone here is his responsibility, end of story."

Layla sighed as she put her mug on the counter. "Aye, I well know that, Ara. But seeing Freya in her dragon form up close may trigger Aimee's beast, and we have no idea how she'll act once she finally comes out."

Holly spoke up. "Then let Aimee see wee Freya from the window first. That way, everything can be contained and monitored. If it goes well, then we can try closer distances until we're confident she can handle Freya in the same room."

Layla eyed the human female. "Not only could the situation regress Aimee at any time, it would eventually endanger Freya."

Holly shrugged. "Everything would be done quite carefully. And we won't know if interacting with Freya will help Aimee or not. Besides, as I heard it, Arabella needed unusual methods herself to fully come out of her shell. Being cautious with Aimee has helped a wee bit, but videos of Freya in her dragon form are the only things that have worked every time, without fail. It's worth a shot."

As Layla glanced between Arabella and Holly, mulling their suggestion, her dragon spoke up. *At least try it through the window. If the experience does have a negative impact, it's better to do it now than months down the line, when it would erase any other kind of progress.*

Layla resisted a mental growl. *I hate guessing and not knowing what will happen. Give me someone in an operating theater, or a sick child, and I know what to do. But the situation with Aimee? I could ruin her life forever with one misstep.*

Her dragon huffed. *Stop it. We're helping. Bloody hell, she started talking for the first time since she was released from the Skyhunter prison. That in and of itself is a huge step and probably one of the greatest tools going forward. I think we can help heal her even more.*

Arabella said, "Well? What does your dragon say?"

Layla looked at the other female askance and muttered, "Of course she's on your side. She almost always is."

Arabella nodded with a smile. "Right, then I'll get to work on Finn. We can wait for one of Aimee's better days to try it."

"Am I even needed here?" Layla drawled.

Holly snorted. "Aye, of course you are. This is a team effort." Before Layla could reply, the human walked up and gently pushed her toward the door. "And whilst we usually love your company, go home. You need some sleep. I know you've been awake for more than a day, Layla. Take care of yourself. Me, Logan, and the others will hold down the fort for a wee while."

At the mention of tiredness, Layla's entire body felt heavy, and any desire to fight it evaporated. Her nursing and support staff were some of the few who knew just how much Layla worked day in and day out. "Just for a bit, to refresh my mind. But make sure to call me if anything comes up, and I mean anything."

"Of course," Holly stated. She pointed toward the exit. "Now, go."

The human only ever ordered Layla around when she needed to rest. And she wasn't going to argue. "Aye, well, I'll see you later."

As she left the cottage, she headed in the direction of the surgery. She was too tired to deal with Chase, so she'd use the room inside the surgery with a bed she'd set up for whenever she needed it.

Her dragon growled. *Coward.*

Ignoring her beast, she somehow made it to the bed, lay down, and instantly fell asleep.

Chapter Four

After installing the necessary equipment in her cottage, Chase had waited for Layla to return. But when she didn't show up for over an hour past finishing the work, he'd gone home to sleep.

And even though the next morning he'd sent a text message asking Layla when she'd like him to come over and explain how the equipment worked, he still hadn't heard back several days later.

She had to be avoiding him.

His dragon spoke up. *She's always busy. She'll contact us when she's ready.*

Such patience from you is a surprise, given how you acted a few nights ago.

It's easier to be patient when Layla isn't right in front of us. Her scent is addicting and makes rational thought go to the wayside.

Which means I'll have to be the adult between the two of us when we finally do see her again.

His beast huffed. *I'm an adult, too. And more often than you are, as a matter of fact.*

Before Chase could reply, he reached his mum's cottage. It was the weekly dinner night he and his brother —and now Grant's mate, too—always attended if possible.

Not wanting his brother to notice something was on his mind, Chase carefully packed away thoughts of Layla. Maybe the dinner was just what he needed to forget about the female for a wee while. After all, it was fun to flirt with his sister-in-law to rile up his older brother. Grant's temper didn't emerge often, but Chase was one of the few who could tempt it out, along with Grant's mate, Faye.

So when he and Faye teamed up against Grant, it was heaven to a younger sibling trying to irritate the older one.

As usual, the front door was unlocked, and he entered the old stone cottage his mother had moved to a little over a year ago. He'd barely taken two steps inside when he heard a familiar female voice, one that wasn't his mother's but Layla's. "I really shouldn't stay, Gillian. I just wanted to stop by and give you the new prescription and check on your headaches. It's my job and pleasure to do it. There's no need to thank me with anything."

His mother's soft voice came down the hall. "It's no bother, lass. I always make quite a bit of food to feed my sons and pregnant daughter-in-law. You could probably feed a small army with all I made and still have leftovers. One more mouth wouldn't make a difference."

On the one hand, Chase couldn't help but smile. Ever since his mother had been spending time with George MacLeod—Arabella's father and an unattached male who had recently moved to Lochguard—she'd been happier and less shy. However, the change meant his mum was currently inviting Chase's true mate to stay for dinner.

If his mum succeeded and Chase had to sit near Layla all evening, then Grant would probably notice the truth rather quickly. His brother was too bloody observant.

And the last thing Chase wanted was to hear advice and caution from his brother. As much as he loved Grant, he and Chase were two very different people, which meant it wasn't a surprise that their true mates were as well. What had worked with Faye wouldn't work with Layla.

He dashed toward the kitchen, but his brother and sister-in-law entered the front door before he could take more than a few steps. Grant's mate, Faye, said, "Och, Chase, you're here already. Come give your favorite sister a hug."

Grant sighed. "You're the only sister he has, and only through mating."

Faye snorted. "I think you've been hanging around with my brothers too much. That sounds like something Fergus would say."

Pasting a smile on his face, Chase turned toward Faye and Grant.

Faye was almost always smiling and full of positive energy. Even though her presence meant he couldn't stop his mother from convincing Layla to stay for dinner, he couldn't be upset with his sister-in-law. If she knew the truth about Layla, she'd no doubt do everything in her power to help him, and then some.

Which would spell trouble before long, despite her good intentions.

After giving her a quick hug, he glanced at his brother. "I'm surprised you're here after me, Mr. Punctual."

Grant grunted, and Faye laughed before saying, "It's my fault. He was, er, helping me with something."

Given how Faye's cheeks flushed, Chase had a feeling he knew what they'd been doing. And very little clothing would've been involved.

His dragon spoke up. *We could be doing that soon with Layla, too, if you only told her the truth.*

Right, and send her running for the hills straight after.

Faye gently shoved Chase down the hall. "Come on, let's go. I'm starving."

"I'd like to tease you about feeding two souls, but you ate this much even before you were pregnant," Chase stated.

"Aye, and I'll do it after as well. MacKenzies love their food, and unlike some, we don't encourage the males to keep eating whilst telling the females to hold back." She raised her chin a fraction. "It's often a free-for-all at my mum's house, but most of the time I win and swipe more food than my brothers. Whilst I don't care if my bairn is a girl or boy, he or she will know how to beat out all her cousins when it comes to dinner time."

Chase grinned at how proud she sounded. "When's

the next MacKenzie dinner then, so I can pay attention and watch your moves? In the past, I always laughed at the food fights."

Grant shoved him. "No more food fights. Last time, Faye got a black eye."

Faye rolled her eyes. "It was a small bruise from a chunk of cheese. I doubt Mum will serve it again, given how you growled and threatened Fraser's bollocks."

Grant narrowed his eyes. "Just because Fraser's mate is no longer pregnant doesn't mean he can forget what it's like to protect one who is. If he provokes me, I'll protect what's mine."

Faye raised an eyebrow at her mate. "I'd like to think I can protect myself against my brother. I did fine for over twenty years before you."

"You weren't pregnant then."

As the pair stared at one another, having some sort of nonverbal conversation, Chase decided he needed to break it up. Usually, the staring ended with his brother issuing an ultimatum or order of some sort—which never worked with Faye, so Chase had no idea why he kept doing it to provoke an argument. So Chase took one hand from each of them and tugged them along. "Come on. Mum is probably waiting for us and will need help with setting the table."

Mentioning how their mother needed help worked. Grant shut his mouth, pulled his grip from Chase's, and placed one hand on Faye's back and the other over her nearly full-term pregnant belly.

His dragon snorted. *He's much more well behaved since he mated Faye.*

Faye's presence helps, aye. But he would never cause Mum distress, mated or not, and you know that.

Ever since their father had abandoned them all a couple of years ago, he and his brother had made a pact to try harder than before to make their mother happy. It didn't always work—Chase liked needling his brother sometimes, which made their mum frown—but they were behaving for the moment.

As they approached the kitchen door, Layla's scent reached his nose. *Fuck.* She was still here.

This was going to be the most difficult dinner of his life. Unlike his brother, Chase wasn't meant to be a soldier or leader who kept emotions in check when needed. Bloody hell, it'd taken everything he'd had to keep the truth of his true mate a secret. He couldn't imagine doing it on a regular basis with every little thing.

His dragon spoke up. *Be your normal self. Everyone in the clan knows you were stopping by to see Layla at work all the time and leaving wee gifts. If you act distant now, Grant will notice that, too.*

He mentally sighed. *Damned if I do, damned if I don't.*

Aye, it seems so. Which is why you should simply tell him the truth and embrace it.

Hush, dragon, or I'll create a mental maze and toss you in there.

I'd dare you, but it's been a few days since we've seen Layla. So I'll behave for now.

His beast fell silent, and Chase entered the kitchen, finding Layla's gaze straight away. He smiled at her before he took in the dark smudges under her eyes and her slightly tousled hair. She'd been working too much again.

The urge to take care of her surged through his body, but Chase resisted. He needed to win her first and then act like her mate and not the other way around. Layla was a dominant female, which required more care.

Of course, Chase was up for the challenge.

LAYLA HAD HOPED to check on Gillian McFarland as quickly as possible and leave before either of her sons showed up. Especially since sometimes her sons came over for dinner, but it wasn't always the same day or time.

If only Layla hadn't had to set one of the children's broken bones in the morning, she might've made the run sooner.

But it hadn't worked out that way. Which was why she now stood in Gillian's kitchen, agreeing to stay for dinner and asking what she could do to help.

Her dragon spoke up. *It'll be fun. And less tense than our family dinners.*

Ever since her sister's radio silence had begun five years ago, the old camaraderie with her parents had all but disappeared after one too many arguments between her and them. Layla couldn't remember the last time they'd even held a conversation longer than a few minutes. *I somehow doubt it'll be less tense or enjoyable. We've been avoiding Chase, and it'll be hard to find the balance of paying attention to him and ignoring him to avoid any special notice from Faye and Grant.*

Her dragon grunted. *Not we, but* you *have been avoiding him. And I made no promise about not flashing naked images of him, either.*

That's unhelpful. Grant and Faye will surely notice if you make me blush.

So? It's not like they'll tell the entire clan.

Layla resisted a sigh. *You see things in black and white, dragon. Faye tells her family almost everything that's unrelated to clan security, and if it slips out and her mum hears about it, who knows what'll happen.*

Faye's mother, Lorna MacKenzie, knew everything about everyone inside Lochguard, to a troubling degree. A wonderfully kind-hearted female who competed for the biggest gossip inside the clan.

However, before Layla could worry more about it, Chase walked casually into the kitchen.

Or, so he was trying to appear. The second his gaze met hers, his pupils flashed, and her heart skipped a beat. The night when they'd been standing close, mere inches apart, came rushing back.

His heat, his scent, his smoldering gaze that had turned her knees weak. The way he'd leaned close, almost as if to kiss her. And how she'd been so close to letting him.

Stop it, Layla. No matter what, no blushing, she reminded herself.

Her dragon sat silently but smugly at the back of her mind.

Chase said, "Hello, Layla. I didn't know you'd be here."

Gillian McFarland went to her son and lightly kissed

his cheek. "I invited her to stay for dinner as a thank you for bringing me my medicine."

Layla swore she saw Gillian wink at her son but brushed it aside. If his mother was trying to matchmake, that would make things even harder.

Her dragon merely laughed.

Determined not to let the world decide her future for her, Layla ignored the mother-and-son pair and turned toward Faye. "Everything's going well with the bairn?"

Faye placed a hand over her large, round abdomen. "Aye, most of the time." Faye stepped closer to whisper, "Although I could do with a break from my randy beast."

Layla bit back a smile. "When a mating is still new— and yours is less than a year old—that tends to happen. Of course, if the mate bond is strong enough, it may never go away."

Faye sighed. "I like a good tumble as much as the next person, but I also like being able to work occasionally, too."

Grant came to Faye's side and murmured, "You don't have to work as much as you do, love. Cooper can help me until the bairn is born."

Faye narrowed her eyes at Grant. "If you think having the doctor here will keep me from sharing my true feelings about being idle for however many months, until you deem me safe enough to work, then you don't know me at all, Grant McFarland."

Grant leaned over to whisper something Layla couldn't hear. As Faye's body relaxed, Layla did, too. While she knew the pair liked to argue and make up repeatedly, the doctor in her couldn't help but worry about their unborn child. Especially since she—only Layla and her nurses knew the gender of the bairn, as per dragon-shifter tradition—could come at any time now, and Layla would prefer not to have to deliver a child with Chase around to distract her.

Her dragon sighed. *Faye will be fine. Don't you start treating her like a porcelain doll, too.*

I won't. But it's my job to think of her health, and sometimes that means the patient has to take it easy, no matter if they're male or female.

Gillian's voice caught her attention. "Layla, do you mind helping Chase with the cutlery? I normally wouldn't ask a guest to do it, but I try to keep the knives away from my eldest son and his mate, lest one of them try to impress the other by tossing it at a target."

Faye grinned. "That was only the one time, Gillian, and I proved my point to Grant. He won't doubt my aim with a blade ever again."

Grant grunted. "And if I could get away with it, I'd make sure we didn't have any knives in the house at all. But given how you like steak currently, that's not going to happen."

Faye smiled sweetly. "We're dragon-shifters, Grant. I'd just use a talon to slice the meat if you ever became that overprotective."

Chase jumped in. "Aye, and I'm sure she's proficient with those as well, brother. If you're having one of your make-up sessions, I'd watch those hands around your bollocks if I were you."

Gillian clicked her tongue. "Chase, stop it. We have a guest, and I'm fairly certain she doesn't want to hear about genitals right before she eats."

Layla's dragon cackled. *Well, maybe if it were about Chase's, then I'd be all ears. Add in his hard cock for us to lick, and that would fill me right up.*

Ignoring her dragon, she turned to Chase and did her best to appear nonchalant. "Where's the cutlery?"

He whispered loudly for dramatic effect. "Clever lass. Let's keep it away from Faye for as long as possible."

Faye growled, but Chase ignored the female, grabbed Layla's hand, and pulled her toward a drawer. Even with three other people watching, she couldn't ignore how his skin against hers sent a rush of heat through her body.

His warm, slightly rough hands that she'd love to have caress every inch of her skin.

No. She couldn't let her thoughts go down that road.

When he finally released her hand, it took everything she had not to snatch it away quickly, as if she'd been burned.

Chase must've noticed something because he instantly raised an eyebrow in question.

She shook her head a fraction, hoping he'd take her hint about leaving well enough alone.

He opened the drawer and started handing her forks and knives. "We'll keep the knives on our side of the table until Faye absolutely needs one." Faye protested with a noise, but Chase continued before she could say a word. "I love you, sister, but whilst my brother, mum, and I are all used to the craziness of your family's dinners, this is

The Dragon's Pursuit

probably the first dinner including a MacKenzie for Layla. I'd rather not have her first include some sort of injury from you trying to knock a roll off Grant's head with a knife like last time."

Layla blinked. "Pardon?"

Faye waved a hand in dismissal. "Grant bet me I couldn't do it, so I proved to him I could. My mate can stand as still as a stone, which most definitely helped."

"Aye, though it's not an experience I'd like to repeat anytime soon," Grant drawled.

As they began recounting the details of said knife-throwing event, Layla tried to follow along. She'd heard the rumors of the MacKenzie dinners, but never any concrete details. If Faye's knife throwing was the tip of the iceberg, maybe she should issue some sort of health warning. Or she could threaten not to treat anyone who was hurt at said dinners to encourage better behavior.

Her dragon laughed. *As if that would work. Not to mention you couldn't let an injured person suffer.*

I should try something, though, as an extra layer of precaution.

No, don't think about work right now. Just try to have fun for once. It won't make up for not giving me enough sex, but at least it'll be a good distraction.

Chase whispered softly into her ear, "Come. They may be at each other for a good hour, and I know for a fact you should eat more. Let's set the cutlery and grab the best bits for ourselves."

Before she could reply, Chase placed a hand on her lower back and guided her into the adjoining dining room.

Considering Layla was usually the one leading others around and offering strength, it was strange to be on the receiving end. Even if Chase wasn't doing it intentionally, his fingers massaged her lower back and released a wee bit of tension with each stroke.

When they were alone inside the small room—which was filled with a large dining table, chairs, and more shelves holding human-shaped knickknacks than Layla had seen anywhere else—Chase quickly shut the door and asked, "Why have you been avoiding me, lass?"

"I haven't," she stated automatically as she tried to step back.

Chase pressed his hand a wee bit firmer into her back, keeping her in place. "You're lying. Don't you want to find out the cause of your problem? The evidence you need may already be available, ready to be watched and noticed."

While she appreciated Chase keeping things vague about someone stealing supplies from the surgery, they only had seconds before someone else would enter. So she said, "I've been extremely busy."

"And?" he asked softly. "Is it related to your comment about how giving in might break you?"

She searched his gaze, surprised at how he remembered her words from the last time they'd been alone together.

Her dragon yawned. *He's observant. Chase may not be a Protector, but he notices everything about us. Maybe even remembers it all, too.*

For the first time, a strange niggling started at the back of Layla's mind.

All the visits, the coffee, the wee gifts from Chase, combined with his determination to win her over despite her attempts to push him away, could make sense. Aye, if she were his true mate, it'd all fit perfectly.

She'd never heard of an older female/younger male pair of true mates before, which was why she'd never considered it. However, it could be possible.

And if so, Chase's dragon should know if they were true mates.

She wanted—no, needed—to learn the truth.

Before she could change her mind, Layla blurted without thinking, "Are we true mates, Chase?"

In the next second, the door clicked closed. *Damn.* Someone had probably just heard her question.

However, in that moment, she didn't care. Instead, she searched Chase's gaze and repeated, "Are we?"

IF GIVEN A CHOICE, Chase would've wanted Layla to know him better before he answered the life-changing question.

However, as Layla searched his eyes and waited for a reply, there was no other real option but to tell the truth or risk losing her forever.

His dragon whispered, *Just tell her.*

Chase nodded. "Aye, my dragon says we're true mates."

Rather than panic, Layla asked calmly, "How long have you known?"

"For over two years."

She closed her eyes and took a deep breath. What he wouldn't give to have her open them and let him see what was going on inside her brain.

Because the next few moments could drastically alter both of their lives.

His dragon grunted. *Then don't stand still. Talk to her, convince her, remind her of how much she responds to our touch.*

Oh, how he wanted to. *She'll probably flee if we do. Give her a few moments, aye?*

We don't have a few moments. The family will enter soon.

Speaking of which, they already should have.

Then he realized the kitchen was quiet, almost too quiet. Not even the smallest shuffle of feet or whisper reached his ears.

If he were a betting male, he'd say they'd all left them after his mum had walked in and rushed right back out.

However, in the next second, Layla opened her dark brown eyes, and he forgot about everything else but the female in front of him.

As he tried to gauge her guarded expression, Layla cleared her throat. "So ever since you hit maturity, your dragon has been telling you to go after me. You never had a chance to grow and discover what kind of lass you truly want for yourself."

Chase had been cautious for years. No more. He growled and leaned closer. "I fought him at first, because I was young and wanted to dally with a few more lasses before settling down. However, it didn't take long for me to notice how clever, kind, and beautiful you are. As time went on, I stopped fighting my dragon. And not because of instinct, but because I wanted you for myself."

Time stilled as she stared into his eyes, her pupils flashing between round and slitted. Odds were that her dragon was on his side. Not every true mate pairing worked or even had dragons on both sides wanting it, but it did more often than not.

And yet, if Layla's human half wasn't on board, too, then nothing would happen. In a worst-case scenario, one of them would be sent to another clan—most likely him—until enough time passed and the true mate pull faded. As long as they didn't kiss each other on the lips and start the need for a mate-claim frenzy, the true mate pull would fade within a few years.

But he didn't want to go away and forget Layla. Over the years, he'd learned how much she needed someone in her life, someone to help share burdens or to bring some laughter into her life. Chase wanted to be that male. He couldn't—or wouldn't—force her, but he wasn't going to give up easily, either.

So he finally asked the question he didn't know the answer to before he decided his next tactic. "What do you want, Layla? Tell me truthfully."

If she tried to step away again, he'd have let her go. Every breath he took made his heart pound harder.

However, she didn't walk away but instead, gingerly placed a hand on his chest. Even through his shirt, the searing heat of her touch made him draw in a breath.

She never broke her gaze as she murmured, "I-I don't know. Rationally, I should laugh and say it'd never work."

He risked raising a hand to lightly trace her jaw, loving how she leaned a little into his caress. "But?"

Her eyes flashed faster as he continued to stroke her soft skin. She replied, "It might be worth a try."

Fuck, what he wouldn't give to kiss her and start trying.

However, he couldn't or he'd start the mate-claim frenzy. So Chase remained where he was, keeping up the steady pace against her jaw. "Then it means you'll let me court you, aye?"

She smiled. "Court is such an old-fashioned term. And yet, it almost fits considering how you can't even kiss me until we decide what to do."

He liked that she used the term "we." Leaning a fraction closer, Chase said, "What are your ground rules? And before you protest, aye, of course you'd have some."

She raised her brows. "Well, of course there needs to be some. After all, I can't just kiss you and let the mate-claim frenzy take over. I have responsibilities, ones that if I don't think about, people could die. Not to mention the result of a frenzy could hurt the clan in the long run, too."

Doing his best to keep his mind free of Layla naked and at his mercy for a sex marathon, as well as her eventually round with their child, he focused on his response. "A child would disrupt your life."

"That's part of it. But there's also the current problem I have at the surgery, which, if left unresolved, could hurt the clan further."

Right, the stolen medical supplies. "I'll help you with that, lass. And I promise—no kissing on the mouth until you want it."

Moving his head even closer, Chase only stopped about an inch from her skin. Her scent was stronger where her neck met her jaw, and if that wasn't already enough to make both man and beast hum, he could also smell her arousal.

His dragon growled. *Then at least kiss her neck, jaw, somewhere.*

He whispered, "Let me kiss your skin, Layla. It might help persuade you to give this more of a chance."

Chase expected her to decline for some rational reason or other, but she tilted her head a fraction. Taking that as a yes, he closed the distance to press his lips to her warm, soft jaw. When she moaned, he lightly traced her jaw with his tongue, down her neck, until he could lightly bite where her neck met her shoulder.

Her hand went to his hair, her nails digging in, making his cock instantly hard.

His dragon roared. *More, taste more of her skin. That small sample isn't nearly enough.*

Chase didn't wait another second to pull Layla's body flush against his, loving how her breasts pressed into his chest, her nipples already hard and straining. Fuck, he wanted to taste one, torture it slowly until his female was about to come. Only because at any moment his family could walk back into the room did he not attempt it.

When Layla's free arm wrapped around his shoulders, he moved back up to her face to kiss her cheek, her nose, her brow. "It's better than I've imagined. So much better." He moved his head to look into her eyes again. The heat there only made him harder. "Tell me how you feel, Layla. Not what you think, but how you feel right here, right now, in my arms."

She murmured, "Warm, wanted, fragile, and so many other things all at once."

Threading his fingers into the back of her hair, he asked, "Tell me why you're fragile, Layla. I hope not because of me. I'd rather cut off my own dick than hurt one hair on your body."

Her lips twitched. "I don't think your dragon would sit back and allow you to cut off your penis."

While he appreciated humor as much as the next person, he wasn't going to allow her to dodge his question. "Aye, I doubt it. But let's get back to the bit about why you feel fragile."

She bit her lower lip a few beats before finally saying, "Not many people push boundaries with me. That is both good and bad, I think." He growled as a reminder of his question, and she added, "Fine. The reason is that while this feels good right now, it doesn't mean it'll last. I work long hours, my schedule is unpredictable, and some days I give so much of myself that I don't have anything left to give someone else at the end of the day. It's not what I'd call a perfect future, and I'm well aware it's one any male would grow tired of eventually. And since I'm not the type of female to date casually and freely give my emotions, it'd break me in the end when a male decided it was too much to handle. It's why I never really tried dating anyone since I first began my medical training, to protect myself."

He hated how she felt the need to distance herself from everyone, to guard her heart. He gently caressed her cheek. "You say that as if I don't already know all of that about you. And as long as you allow me to take care of you on those days when you're too exhausted to do more than eat and sleep, then it'd be enough for me." He searched her eyes before adding, "I wouldn't leave you, Layla."

Chase knew what it was like to have someone who should love you just leave one day and never come back.

Her brows came together. "Saying the words is one thing, but it's much harder in real life, Chase. Usually only other doctors or nurses understand how draining this profession can be, and they know how to handle the demands of it."

If Layla believed actions more than words, Chase would do just that. "Then give me a trial period. I can secretly stay with you most days and nights, help you solve the mystery of the surgery, and prove I can be the mate of a dragon doctor."

While living in the same cottage as Layla for even a short amount of time without kissing her would be difficult, Chase had survived two fucking years of not having her. He could wait a little longer.

She finally said, "People will talk, aye? And this being Lochguard, everyone will try to meddle, which will only make things harder than they're going to be already."

He shook his head. "They won't find out if I can help it. I'll be careful. I wasn't what you'd call the most well-behaved teenager. Not to mention when I was doing my initial electrician's training in Inverness, I became a master of leaving the boarding house after curfew to explore the surrounding areas and always made it back unnoticed." He winked. "I never even received a warning."

"The doctor in me wants to scold that behavior."

"But?"

Her lips curled upward. "But if it's true, it may be helpful to our situation."

Chase loved how the situation had become theirs so quickly.

Maybe he did have a chance with Layla after all. After two years of holding back, it was almost too much to hope for.

His dragon spoke up. *Of course we have a chance with her. Now, focus on making her say yes so we can kiss her skin again.*

I'm not sure I could make her do anything.

His beast growled. *Try harder.*

"Chase? What does your dragon say?" Layla asked.

He snorted. "He's excited, is all. As you well know, inner dragons aren't the most patient lot. And for you to even consider giving us a chance is a massive deal to him." He moved a finger to trace the outer edge of her ear. "So, will you give us a chance? Even if it's only a couple of weeks or a month, I'll treat every day as if it were our last, and give it my everything."

Lifting her hand from his chest, she lightly brushed her fingers against his cheek. The light touch sent another rush of heat through his body.

And she'd only touched his face. He'd explode when her fingers finally wrapped around his cock and squeezed.

Fuck, he'd promise her anything to make that a reality.

She murmured, "There are a million reasons why I should say no."

"But?" he prodded gently.

She searched his gaze and brushed a stray lock of hair off his forehead. "But I can't bring myself to say anything but yes."

His heart rate kicked up. "When can we start?" he croaked.

He swore she leaned more against him as she replied, "Tomorrow, after I finish work? That'll give me time to tidy up a bit. There are a few things I'd rather you not see lying about my house."

He tightened his arm around her waist. "Och, lass, now all I'll be doing is thinking of what those forbidden items are."

She grinned, her eyes crinkling at the corners and only making her even more beautiful to him. "Then maybe that can be your incentive to stick around."

Moving his face closer, he stopped a few inches from her lips. "All the incentive I need is standing right here in front of me."

Her breath hitched, and it took every iota of restraint he possessed not to close the distance and kiss her.

He wondered if older dragonmen could better restrain themselves around their true mates.

His dragon snorted. *I doubt it.*

It was then he heard the front door open and close, followed by Faye's voice. "I'm hungry and tired of waiting. And you know that once I smell something as delicious as a roast and potatoes, I can't even imagine eating anything else."

Layla stepped away and he let her go. She whispered, "This is our secret, aye? Promise me."

As much as he wanted to scream to the world that Layla was allowing him to court her, he nodded. "I promise."

She quickly added, an eager gleam in her eye, "I can't wait until tomorrow evening."

Before he could reply, Faye burst through the door, carrying the roast on a plate. "Sorry for the delay. I just needed a wee bit of fresh air."

Since he didn't want to arouse any suspicion— although he suspected his mum and possibly Faye and Grant already knew the truth—Chase replied, "And you took the others with you?"

"Of course. I'm in a delicate condition, aye? I needed at least two people around in case I fainted."

Grant entered the room, snorting. "You're about as delicate as a brick wall."

Faye narrowed her eyes. "The knives are right there, Grant. Tempt me to reach for one of them."

Grant smiled. "You wouldn't hurt me, love."

"No, but it would most definitely boost morale with the Protectors if I tried hitting things off your head with a knife as a limited run show."

His mother entered, a bowl of potatoes in her hands. "Aye, aye, you two could entertain the entire clan for years if you wished. But for now, it's supper time. And I will separate you two if you can't behave."

"Now you're sounding like my mum," Faye muttered.

Chase stole a quick glance at Layla, and the amusement in her eyes was clear even from where he was standing.

In all the years he'd been watching her from afar, he hadn't seen much of it there.

Which meant he'd have to rectify that, in addition to proving he could be a dragon doctor's mate.

The next evening couldn't come soon enough.

Chapter Five

The following day, Layla had more trouble than usual concentrating on her work. It wasn't as bad when she talked or visited with patients, but the second she was alone in her office, her mind wandered to Chase and the deal she'd made with him.

Which was why she currently sat at her desk, unfinished paperwork in front of her, and tried her best not to relive him pulling her close and kissing her skin from the night before.

Her dragon huffed. *It's nearly time to leave. But we can't do that until you finish the last patient's notes.*

Maybe some doctors would put it off to the following day, but the notes in question were about Gina MacDonald-MacKenzie. And since the female was not only human but also pregnant with twins—the MacKenzies seemed to be cursed or blessed with them in abundance —Layla always wanted to ensure the notes were complete in case something happened and she wasn't there to provide crucial facts straightaway.

She replied to her beast, *Then don't distract me with memories whilst I work and finish this up.*

I haven't distracted you much today. It's been all on your own. I think deep down, you've wanted him for a while, too. And now we're closer to having him, you let yourself dream.

Her dragon may be correct, but Layla wasn't going to admit it right then and there. True, she'd thought about Chase's lips on her skin, the hardness of his chest, the way he held her possessively against him. But she'd also replayed his ease at dinner, the way he teased his brother endlessly, and how he tried his hardest to make his mother laugh.

Most people probably wouldn't have noticed, but Layla had been treating Gillian for years. To see Chase try so hard to make his mum happy only raised her opinion of him.

Of course thinking about his smiles, his wit, and his panty-melting touches wouldn't help her get her work done. So with herculean effort, Layla focused on the patient file and filling in all the details. Since it had been a routine examination, it didn't take long to finish.

As soon as she did, Layla stood, shrugged out of her lab coat, and picked up her bag. However, she paused at the door and took a few deep breaths. Layla never rushed around unless it had to do with a patient or some kind of emergency. If she started dashing from the surgery at quitting time, someone would notice and start asking questions.

Questions she didn't want to answer until she felt more comfortable about what to say.

Although if Chase wasn't able to get in and out of her cottage unnoticed, she would have to start taming clan gossip, which would be even worse.

Her dragon grunted. *You worry too much. I have faith in Chase and his ability to sneak into our place unnoticed. After all, if he managed to watch us for two whole years and keep his dragon in check, then he's a lot stronger than most males his age.*

You just want to get naked with him sooner rather than later. So of course you'd plead his case.

No, if I didn't think he'd be a strong enough male, I'd say so. Remember, female dragons are usually more leery of a potential true mate than males. He still has to win me over, too.

Aye, I hope you won't accept him straightaway without knowing him better. For me, there's a lot to do and sort through before I can give him any sort of long-term answer.

Her dragon's voice softened. *Just don't doom the relationship before it even begins.*

True, Layla had done so before. Anytime a male had wanted to see her more, know her better, and even started to kindle feelings inside her, Layla had found excuses to end it. Mostly it centered around her career— training to be a dragon-shifter doctor wasn't an easy thing—but she'd seen many a bad mating over the years in her role and how it could devastate people.

Her own parents were comfortable in the present with each other but had fallen out of love long ago. Add in her sister's arranged mating and ensuing disappearance, and Layla's was skeptical about true love.

Her dragon chimed in again. *You say that but look at the*

MacKenzies. Not to mention Finn and Arabella. Even Alistair and Kiyana. They've all overcome so much to be together and stay together. Why can't we find the same?

Just because they found it doesn't mean we automatically will get it, too.

Her dragon huffed. *You're too rational for your own good.*

Someone has to be.

Layla exited her office and made her way toward the side door used for staff. To her relief, she only had to answer one question on the way out before she reached the cool, winter air.

The Scottish Highlands in winter were dark, cold, and wet. But as Layla's feet crunched against the light snow on the ground, she didn't mind. The darkness meant most of the clan retreated to their homes once the sun went down and she could enjoy a sense of peace she rarely found when working.

It wasn't long before she reached the front door of her cottage, unlocked it, and stepped inside. A light glow came from the kitchen, and she moved toward it, wondering if Chase had invited himself in unannounced.

She gasped when she reached the doorway.

Lit candles sat around the tables and counter, a dim glow filling the space. At the center was her small table, crammed with different pizza boxes and several bags of her favorite sweets. If that wasn't good enough, Chase stood behind a chair and motioned for her to come over.

Somehow she made her feet work and said, "No one knows my secret love of pizza. I only make it from scratch, and always eat it alone."

As he slid the chair under her, he leaned down and

whispered, "As I mentioned, I've spent two years watching the female I couldn't have. During which, I had a lot of time to learn what you liked."

He slid into the seat next to her, and she raised an eyebrow. "That sounds a wee bit creepy, if I'm honest."

Making a cross over his heart, he replied, "I never ventured into creepy territory, I promise. Because when I finally see your naked body, I want you to look right into my gaze and show me every emotion you have."

Her heart skipped a beat at the certainty in his words. With anyone else, she'd probably scold him to behave.

But as wetness rushed between her thighs, Layla shivered at the thought of Chase's intense, dark gaze watching her undress.

Bloody hell, what have I become?

Her dragon snorted but remained silent.

Chase's heated gaze morphed into an inquiring one. "Is today one of the days you need only food and bed?"

There he went again, remembering what she'd said. She shook her head. "No. Today was a short day for me, really."

"Ten hours shouldn't be short," he growled.

She shrugged as she opened a pizza box—noting that they came from the nearest human town—and took a slice of pepperoni pizza. Her mouth watered at the scent of seasoned meat and cheese. "It usually doesn't get much shorter. Although, tomorrow the Seahaven doctor is coming for the first time, so maybe I'll get off work a little earlier."

Chase took some food for himself. "Are you nervous about him coming?"

A few people had asked her that question, including Lochguard's clan leader. She'd been mostly honest with Finn, only leaving out her own constant, protective worry of the clan. However, she didn't hesitate to answer Chase. Maybe because he was outside her usual sphere of work and responsibilities. "More than I'd like. By all accounts, Daniel Keith is a good doctor. And aye, he used to live on Lochguard, but I didn't really know him back then to judge his character. Regardless, it's my duty to watch over the clan's health. And until I can judge his skills, I'm not sure of how much help he'll truly be since I'll be watching him instead of doing work myself."

Chase nodded. "Aye, I can understand needing to assess and judge his skills. It's why they didn't let me wire an entire building by myself on the first day of my training, and only once I passed muster. It'll take time, but I'll be rooting for him to far exceed your expectations. It's not purely for altruistic reasons, mind you." He leaned over and added, "I'll always crave more alone time with you."

She rolled her eyes. "You can stop being over the top at any time now, Chase. You already have me sitting here with you, so no need to flirt."

He took her free hand and brought her knuckles to his lips. The light touch caused electricity to race through her body.

As they stared at one another, his gaze intent and heated, she stopped breathing for a few seconds.

Bloody hell, she'd never been so attuned to a male before.

He murmured, "You deserve to be flirted with. Besides, it's not something I can easily turn off."

She raised her brows. "I hope you're not going to regale me with your former conquests."

He leaned even closer until she felt his breath on her cheek. "Fuck, Layla, don't do that. Right here, right now, it's just us. I don't want to talk about other males or females. I want to know you, lass, and only you."

Her dragon spoke up. *He means it, I can tell. Stop trying to push him away already.*

At her dragon's words, she resisted a sigh. *I promise I don't try to do it deliberately.*

Don't tell me. Talk to him.

Chase watched her, waiting. Unused to speaking freely about her thoughts, it took Layla a second to say, "Sorry. It's just unreal still, aye? You being here, looking at me like that."

He smiled, humor in his eyes. "Like what?"

"You know what."

He gently ran his thumb over her knuckles. "No, I don't. Enlighten me, lass. I can be a bit thick at times when it comes to females."

She narrowed her eyes and Chase waggled his eyebrows. She couldn't help but laugh. "You're incorrigible."

Kissing her hand again, he murmured, "I'm still waiting for you to describe this look I have."

For most of the last seventeen years, ever since she'd started her medical training at eighteen, Layla had learned to hold back part of herself in order to do her work. Yet, as she stared into Chase's eyes, she realized how much she wanted to be able to say whatever came to mind. So, for the first time in a long time, she did. "You keep looking at me as if I'm the only female in the world, and that you'd like nothing better than to eat me up."

In a flash, Chase tugged her into his lap and held her close. With his strong arms around her, his solid chest against her side, and even his arousal pressing against her outer thigh, her entire body was on fire, aching to have more than just an embrace.

Layla was starting to understand how a mate-claim frenzy had begun as an afterthought, if all true mates had the same chemistry as she and Chase.

Not that chemistry was enough, she reminded herself.

Chase nuzzled his nose against her cheek as he said, "Your assessment of my look is correct." He moved his mouth to her ear, his hot breath tickling her with each syllable. "And it's not going to fade anytime soon, so get used to it."

She snorted. "If I didn't know this clan so well, I'd dare you to keep looking at me like that for as long as possible."

He moved to catch her gaze again, a smile on his lips. "And because you know the clan so well?"

Without thinking, she moved a finger to trace the bridge of his nose. "Because I do, I know your stubbornness would try to see it through, no matter what, especially if a bet was involved. And then our secret wouldn't be one anymore, would it?"

"I don't need a bet to keep looking at you like I do, Layla."

The truth in his words did something to her heart.

Neither

"How can you be so certain of that? Neither of us had parents with some happily-ever-after love story. Love and wanting can fade, Chase. It happens all the time."

She expected him to deflect and change the subject, but he searched her eyes as he said, "Aye, both of our parents' happy endings didn't last. But their stories aren't ours, and we can make our own, lass. Even given how much of a bastard my father was to my mum when he abandoned her, there are people out there like Lorna MacKenzie, who loved her mate for nearly thirty years after his death."

"It's easier to stay in love with someone if they remain a memory."

He tucked a section of hair behind her ear. "What's made you so cynical, Layla? Tell me."

Chase was asking for even more of herself. She shifted in her seat, debating what to do. No one knew the full extent of her sister's silence, not even the clan leader. Her mother was determined to pretend everything was normal, and her father had agreed. After the second or third year, Layla had lacked the energy to keep fighting them as she became head doctor.

So telling Chase would be a bloody big deal.

Her dragon spoke softly. *You're doing it again. How can he get to know us if you don't share things?*

She finally met Chase's eyes again. At the patience and curiosity burning in them, she finally blurted, "What do you know about my younger sister, Yasmin?"

CHASE HAD KNOWN that Layla put on a façade to be the clan doctor, showing a certain side of herself to everyone.

However, despite his years of watching her, not even he had realized how little she talked of herself until this evening.

Some males might be upset at all the hesitating and attempts at deflection. But to Chase, it only made him more curious. And not just because he wanted to become the one she leaned on, either. The more he learned about Layla MacFie, the hungrier he grew to know even more. Aye, she was a doctor, but there was so much more to her, he was certain. And he was starting to think he'd do anything to bring out that other side of her, the one she kept from everyone else.

He watched Layla, waiting for an answer to his question about being cynical. When she finally looked up, she asked, "What do you know about my younger sister, Yasmin?"

The sister. Rumors ran aplenty, but he preferred the truth instead. So he answered, "Not much. I vaguely remember her sending-off party at the great hall, but that was what, four or five years ago?"

Layla bobbed her head. "Aye, too long ago."

The sadness in her voice instantly made both man and beast alert. "What about her, lass? What happened to your sister to make you so cynical?"

She looked at his chest and plucked at his top. She may be in her thirties, but in that moment, she barely looked older than twenty. She said softly, "My mother arranged a marriage for Yasmin to a friend's son in Clan One in Iran—the clans are simply numbered there. And since Yasmin was always the dutiful one, desperate for our parents' approval, she agreed to it despite me being the only one who knew she cared for someone here."

He resisted a frown. Arranged matings had been rare for the last fifty or hundred years among dragon-shifters. And if there had been someone on Lochguard who loved her, then they'd been a bloody fool to let Yasmin go without a fight. Doing his best to keep his voice calm, he asked, "Why do you think she agreed to it?"

Layla shrugged, still keeping her gaze on his chest. "I don't know. I think Yas was always trying to convince herself it was what she wanted, that it would make Mum proud, and so she never complained or shed a tear, at least that I know of."

Chase had heard maybe two real complaints from Layla over the last two years. "So, she's like you, then."

Her startled gaze met his. "Why would you say that?"

He smiled as he stroked her back, hoping to calm her. "Come, lass, you don't complain, either. And there's plenty to go on about, especially given how much you have to put up with here. Archie and Cal alone are enough to make one take up drinking."

The corner of her lips curled upward, no doubt remembering one of the foolish revenge acts the two old males had carried out over the years, each accusing the other of stealing some of their land or livestock. "They've calmed down quite a bit since becoming involved with Meg Boyd and rarely end up at the surgery anymore."

He snorted. "How that female managed to catch two males, I'll never understand, let alone the rumors about them all sharing a bed together."

Amusement danced in her eyes. "I would elaborate on that, but I'm sworn to secrecy as their doctor."

He gently chucked under her chin. "I don't care about the old biddy and her males. But one day, I'll ferret out all your secrets, Layla. Wait and see."

After a beat, Layla tried to get off his lap and Chase let her. As much as he wanted to act like a possessive male, hold her tight, and say she was going to stay with him, he'd give her some breathing room. For now.

Layla took a bite of pizza, picked up her plate, and motioned toward the hall. "Show me how to view the security footage and then we can watch it together."

Inwardly, he groaned. Watching people coming and going from various storage closets wasn't his idea of an ideal date. And yet, this was only the first of many tests to come when it came to being the mate of a doctor.

Even though he'd have said yes anyway, he stood and tilted his head. "We do that and then I get to pick our next activity."

Chase slowly looked up and down her body, taking in every curve and valley.

Her cheeks flushed and his inner dragon took notice. *There's a lot we can do without kissing her on the mouth.*

Ignoring his beast, he put on a mock expression of surprise. "Why, Dr. MacFie, are you thinking dirty thoughts?"

Her cheeks turned even redder, and he did his best not to laugh. Especially once she stood taller and straightened her shoulders. "Of course not."

Biting back a grin, he crossed over to her, snagging a pizza box on the way. He stopped next to her, leaned over, and whispered, "Don't worry, I have enough dirty thoughts for the both of us, lass."

Her breath hitched, and it took everything he had not to turn his head and kiss her.

Instead, he went down the hall toward the extra bedroom Layla used as a secondary office, where he'd set up the receiving equipment. Part of him wanted to discover the thief right away to ease Layla's worries. However, another part of him wished she'd get bored at seeing nothing suspicious so he could do something to try and make her laugh or smile and help her forget for a few minutes that she was a doctor.

Chase's dragon spoke up. *What happened to all of your patience?*

It's easier to wait when you have no encouragement. Now, however, being around her all the time, it's a lot harder.

If I can keep myself in check, you can, too. We need to prove we're the mate she needs.

Knowing that his dragon was right, Chase hurried toward the office. He'd waited two years for Layla. A few more weeks or months shouldn't be impossible.

No, it had to be possible because he couldn't risk the alternative. If he forced the mate-claim frenzy on Layla, she'd never forgive him.

With a fresh surge of determination coursing through his body, he went after Layla.

Chapter Six

If any other male had said those words to her, about having enough dirty thoughts for the both of them, Layla would've frowned and told them to mind their manners.

But when Chase said them, her body heated, and she itched to asked him what some of them were.

As soon as he left the kitchen, her dragon spoke up. *Then ask him.*

I...can't. He's distracted me enough tonight as it is. And we really need to view that security footage because the longer the supplies keep being stolen, the more it hurts the clan in the long run.

Her dragon huffed. *We can do both. It'd be even easier, though, if you asked for help. Chase's brother would help. And you can't use any excuses because Grant knows how to keep a secret.*

From Finn? I doubt it. The surgery is my domain, and Finn will disrupt it, as well as make everyone question my authority and ability to run the place. I'll ask for help once I know who it is and why they're doing it, but not before.

It wasn't as if Layla would never ask for help if she truly needed it. But no one was dying or in danger. Yet. She wasn't about to become the female who cried wolf.

Her dragon paused a second before adding, *You've proven yourself as head doctor. There's no need to keep shouldering all the burden.*

It's not by choice, dragon. Until another fully trained doctor is around, it has to be this way. I can't entrust a junior one still in training without the necessary supervision. No matter how good their intentions, someone could still die.

Her beast sniffed. *Hand over the smaller duties to the junior doctors, all of them if possible. That alone will free up some time.*

There's not much more I can hand over.

Her dragon was about to reply, but not wanting to have the same argument she'd had many times before with her beast, Layla ignored her and went to her home office.

Right after she sat down, Chase followed suit and took another slice of pizza. Watching Chase casually sitting there, taking a bite of pizza, gave her a glimpse of what an ordinary, everyday life could be. Aye, some females dreamed of flowers, presents, and ballads, but for Layla, she simply wanted a partner in life she could love and be loved by in return, one who would be there for her after a long day of surgeries or paperwork.

She wasn't entirely convinced yet that Chase could be that person, but she was at least giving them a chance. She owed him that much.

She adjusted her position in the chair next to him and her arm casually brushed his. Even so, a slight shock tingled up her skin, making her heart beat faster.

Chase leaned closer toward her. She wondered if he'd touch her again, but he reached around and flipped on a few switches before moving back and typing something on a keyboard. Images appeared on the screen in front of them.

Tamping down her disappointment at him doing exactly what she'd asked, she listened to him explain how to turn it on. Once she nodded at the end, he put the image on fast-forward and ordered, "Eat."

If she weren't so bloody hungry, she'd fight him. But as her stomach growled, she took a bite of the warm, cheesy goodness, loving the grease and ignoring the doctor in her that said she should be eating something healthier.

Chase merely sat and watched her until she'd eaten the entire slice. Once she lifted her plate and made an overdramatic gesture of it being empty, he grinned. "Good, lass."

She rolled her eyes. "I'm not a dog or horse."

He placed another slice on her plate. "No, but since I can't reward you the way I want, I've resorted to teasing you."

Not wanting to flush yet again and only make them both frustrated, Layla asked, "What's one of your guilty pleasures then? You know my secret love of pizza, but what's yours?"

He blinked, surprised at the change of topic. Both woman and beast felt a thread of warmth at being able to surprise the charming male.

She may be predictable at her job, but when she was younger, she'd loved playing pranks on her sister.

Before she could go down memory lane and feel sad again, Chase shrugged and garnered her full attention. "It's not really a secret, but not many people would guess I like gardening and trying to find new plants from around Scotland to plant in my secret garden. Something about taming a yard, working hard to showcase its hidden, unrealized beauty satisfies me. Besides,"—he winked—"it gives me the chance to take off my shirt and have everyone ogle me."

She narrowed her eyes at the thought of a pack of females watching Chase's powerful, sweaty back.

Then she remembered a minor detail. "You said it was secret, so no one would be there to watch you. Unless you count the squirrels and hedgehogs?"

He grinned. "You're too clever for your own good."

Ignoring his comment, she said, "I like that idea. Sort of like a Snow White in reverse, aye? Do you call the animals and they come to help you with the chores? That would be quite the show."

Gently taking her cheek, he nipped her jaw. "Cheeky lass. No bloody animals come when I call."

Teasing Chase was more fun than she'd had in a long time. So she chanced pushing him a wee bit more. "Of course you'd say that, to protect your male pride. But if I found your garden and crouched low, waiting for you to take off your shirt and get to work, I'm sure I'd find a songbird landing on your shoulder within seconds."

His voice was deliciously deep and husky when he murmured, "Is that supposed to embarrass me? Because to have your eyes on my back, och, that would be heaven, lass."

Searching his gaze, she saw the truth there, along with a flicker of heat. Any clever retort she'd had died on her lips. Instead, her cheeks flushed hotter than before, as she imagined him toiling in a garden, wiping sweat from his brow, and then finally tossing a bucket of water over his head. Of course he'd shake it from his hair afterward, a few of the droplets splashing across her face.

It may be winter and too bloody cold for such a fantasy, but a female could dream.

Tracing her jaw, his grin returned. "I'd pay a fortune for your thoughts just now, Layla MacFie. Anything that makes you blush so furiously must be dirty indeed."

As she tried to think of how to reply to *that*, something caught Chase's attention on the screen, and Layla turned to watch.

Someone had entered one of the storage closets. Chase slowed the footage to normal speed, and Layla gasped. "That's Logan."

"Wait, what? Logan likes to tease, but he's an honorable male. I can't imagine he'd steal."

Layla placed her plate to the side and studied the monitor again. Sure enough, Logan plucked a few vials of dragon hormones from one shelf, as well as a bottle of medication used to help with heart arrhythmia from another.

Once Logan left the closet in the video, Chase stopped the footage. He then flipped through the other camera views, looking for any other thefts for about an hour before and after the pilfering they'd noticed. However, Logan never appeared in any of the other frames.

Chase finally turned off the screen, and Layla's frown deepened. Logan Lamont was the nurse she relied on the most heavily, one she never would've imagined betraying her like this.

It took her a second to speak again. "Why wouldn't Logan come and talk to me? If he needed help, surely he knew I'd give it if I could."

"Maybe he can't risk it," Chase murmured. His next words were at a normal volume. "What are you going to do, Layla?"

Sighing, she shrugged. "Confront him privately, I suppose. Although I'll make sure it happens inside the surgery, to help contain the situation."

"Aye, you could. Although he might try to run if you do, even if you're surrounded by other staff. For all we know, his reason for stealing is more important than the consequences he could suffer."

Her dragon chimed in. *Maybe it's for a mate?*

I can't imagine Logan hiding that from me.

Maybe if it was a human or exiled dragon-shifter, he might.

Those drugs wouldn't work on a human and would end up killing them. Logan knows that.

Chase's voice interrupted her inner conversation. "We could ask my brother for help if you want."

Layla met Chase's brown eyes again. "But won't he tell Finn? And then they'll all wonder why I didn't just say something before, not understanding that I wanted to try and contain the situation inside my surgery first."

"Grant would only tell Finn if the situation ends up being a threat to the clan as a whole." He took her hand and squeezed. "But what are the reasons someone might take those things? Knowing that may give me a better way to try to help you."

Glancing at her lap, she wanted to tell him anything he asked. And yet, admitting it aloud would be tantamount to saying she couldn't handle her job as head doctor.

Her beast growled. *That's bloody ridiculous. He won't think less of us. So stop holding back.*

Before she could convince herself not to, she stated, "The only reason someone would steal those items was if they sold them to someone else, or…"

She paused, not wanting to voice her fear.

Chase's warm hand squeezed hers again. "Or what, lass?"

She met Chase's gaze once more. "Or he could be giving them to the exiled dragon-shifters."

Chase's brown eyes turned impassive. "As far as I know, Logan didn't have any family or friends desert him when the exiles left rather than stand with Finn."

Unlike Chase, whose own father and uncle had done so.

In that instant, Layla understood why his eyes had turned blank at the mention of the exiles. He was trying to contain his own emotions. Even if Michael McFarland was the bastard who'd abandoned his family, he was still Chase's father. And him leaving had hurt the male next to her.

The teasing male had his own pain, and Layla had been selfishly forgetting that. She knew better than many that a smile could hide a lot.

And it was time for Layla to stop being selfish, trying

to make her surgery and staff seem perfect and problem-free. Logan's actions could affect a lot of people in the long run.

Squeezing the hand in hers, she said gently, "Regardless if Logan didn't have any friends or family leave, there's always a possibility that a potential true mate did. All of this is becoming more than I can handle, even with your help. So let's go to your brother, Chase. Grant will know what to do."

Nodding, he stood up, taking Layla with him. "Aye, Grant will think of the next steps. And I don't care what he's doing right now. He's going to see us."

Before she knew it, they'd both put on coats and were walking briskly toward Grant and Faye's cottage.

Layla kept waiting for an overwhelming sense of failure to fall over her. However, something about Chase's presence at her side and his hand in hers made her hopeful. Maybe things would work out okay in the end.

Her former boss's departure had been rather sudden, meaning Layla had never had time to ask Gregor all the questions she'd had. True, he always said she could call anytime.

And yet, she'd wanted to prove herself.

However, Layla began to think that the key to being a successful head doctor was being able to rely on others. And she'd never forget that she had Chase to thank for making her realize that insight.

Without thinking, she held his hand even tighter, almost afraid he'd run and leave her alone again. Alone to fight her battles, run her surgery, and to keep her true self hidden from the clan.

Even though it'd only been a short while, that thought scared her. Somehow Chase McFarland had made an impact on her life already.

What she'd said a few nights ago, about breaking in the end if the relationship didn't work out, was more true than ever.

Glancing at Chase's profile, she only hoped his determination turned out to be strong enough. Because aye, she wanted him. And more than for one night, too.

Chapter Seven

C hase rarely asked his brother for help. Not because he didn't trust Grant, or know his older brother would do anything to keep him safe, but rather because Grant had spent most of their childhood doing exactly that.

Their father had been working all the time when they were kids, and he'd often been away for weeks at a time on some job or another. Grant had been the one to grow up quickly and try to help take care of Chase and their mum. It was only when he was older that Chase had learned of the lengths Grant and their mother had gone to raise him and keep him happy.

Namely, by keeping his father's shite behavior secret for as long as possible.

Ever since learning that fact, Chase had done his bloody best to take care of problems on his own and not burden his brother as an adult.

However, Chase wasn't stupid enough to let his pride

get in the way regarding the whole situation with Logan. His brother's entire life focused on two things— protecting his family and his clan. Grant had all the skills Chase lacked to find out what Logan was doing, and it would be idiotic to not call on them.

The thought of his friend stealing didn't sit right. Chase and Logan had been friends their whole lives. Aye, they'd gotten into trouble when they'd been younger, like most dragon-shifters. However, nothing to suggest he'd sell drugs for money or help those who had hurt the clan. Layla had suggested his potential true mate might've been made to flee with her family. However, Chase wasn't so sure about that given how his friend dated and charmed females on a regular basis.

His dragon spoke up. *There's no point speculating about why he's doing it. I'm sure Grant will have the answers within a day or two.*

I hope so. Chase stole a glance at Layla, noting how pale her face was. *Layla will probably blame herself for this, and I don't like her in distress.*

Aye, maybe she should've said something to Finn or Grant or Faye. However, she can't control everything that happens. Maybe she's learned that.

Even so, I think she believes she could have solved it all herself, if only she'd tried harder.

Because Layla always tried her hardest with anything that'd come her way over the last two years and had almost always succeeded.

Her strength and determination had made him wary at first, had made him doubt their age differences. Could he ever match her when she had so many years more experience than him?

However, as months went by, he'd slowly noticed she had faults and weaknesses like anyone did. And it'd made him realize that he didn't need to match her, only complement her. And over time, he'd noticed how well he could do that.

Faye and Grant's cottage came into sight, the front window glowing with light. Good, they were home and he didn't have to waste time trying to find out where they were. Especially since the quick text message he'd sent, asking where they were, had gone unanswered.

Not because his brother was ignoring him, but probably was merely busy with his mate as it was late at night, and Grant's second-in-command would be in charge of the Protectors until morning.

His dragon huffed. *I still say we should've called over and over again, until he picked up.*

This way is quicker, as I said it would be.

Chase said to Layla, "They have a secure room in their place, one where no one can listen in, no matter how hard they try. Wait until we get inside it before saying anything, aye?"

She nodded but said nothing else.

Chase hated her being so silent. If there weren't mere feet from the doorstep, he would've said something to make her frown with irritation or to smile. Anything to help lighten the mood.

He'd just have to do it later, once this was settled.

They arrived at the door. As much as he wanted to barge in, Chase wasn't going to risk finding his brother and sister-in-law naked and moaning in front of them. He pounded on the door and kept at it until it swung open, revealing Grant's furrowed brow and wearing nothing but a pair of pajama bottoms. "What the hell do you want at this hour?" Before Chase could say a word, Grant's gaze moved to Layla and softened. "What happened, Layla? Don't deny it—it's written all over your face."

Chase took Layla's hand again and pushed inside. "Not until we're secure."

Faye had come into the hall, a robe wrapped around her body. But rather than ask questions, she motioned toward the stairs. "Then let's hurry."

In less than a minute, all four of them were inside a spare bedroom that had been turned into a soundproofed meeting room of sorts, one that was also protected from any sort of listening device. Once the door clicked closed, Grant prodded again. "What happened?"

Layla spoke without hesitation, her voice strong. "Someone has been stealing items from the surgery."

Faye tilted her head. "For how long?"

"Nearly a month. And aye, I should've come to you straightaway. But I was afraid that if any of the Protectors started sniffing around, it would make the thief flee, and I'd never discover who it was." She gestured to Chase. "So I asked Chase to help me."

Grant's look was enough of a question, and Chase answered, "I installed hidden security cameras for her. And tonight while watching the footage, we found out who it is."

Faye leaned against Grant's side. "Who?"

"Logan Lamont."

Faye frowned. "Are you sure? Logan hasn't done anything irresponsible since his brother disappeared years ago, without a word."

Layla nodded. "I agree, it doesn't seem like him, but it's him in the footage, plain as day." She recapped what she saw in the footage before adding, "Regardless of our assumptions, the medication he took is very specific and expensive, just like the old monitoring equipment that also went missing recently."

A thought crossed Chase's mind. "Did Logan's brother have a heart condition?"

Layla shook her head. "No, not many dragon-shifters do. And this stays in this room, but the only ones that have been part of Lochguard in the last decade and have heart arrhythmias are Cal, young Ollie, and…"

Her voice trailed off, her face becoming even paler. Not caring that Faye and Grant were there, he cupped her cheek and forced Layla to look at him. He asked gently, "And who, lass?"

She searched his eyes as she whispered, "My sister."

TIME STILLED as a flicker of hope sparked in Layla's chest. There were many more reasons as to why it was impossible that Logan was helping Yasmin, almost too many to count.

And yet, maybe Yasmin had been silent for a reason. They'd never formally received news of her mating ceremony, let alone any updates.

Not even her mother's friends had mentioned something going awry. Or, if they had, her parents had
become fantastic liars, which would almost be worse. If
her sister had been missing for years and they hadn't said
a word, Layla wasn't sure she could forgive them.

Her dragon said, *Maybe they were trying to keep a secret,
one that could harm the clan as a whole. It doesn't mean they were
trying to lie to us.*

Perhaps, Layla muttered.

Her dragon added, *Or, for all we know, our parents were
ordered to be silent.*

You're too bloody optimistic, dragon.

*Regardless of all that, even a wee chance of Yasmin being
nearby is better than zero.*

Before Layla's mind could go down the road of how
Yasmin could possibly be back in Scotland, Grant spoke.
"Rather than speculate on who Logan is helping, let's just
talk to him, aye? Is he on duty tonight, Layla?"

She nodded. "His shift won't end for another two
hours."

Faye jumped in. "Then I think it's time for me to
complain of contractions and make a visit."

Grant searched his mate's gaze. "You're only acting,
aye?"

Faye smiled. "Of course. Once the contractions hit,
you'll know, Grant McFarland. Believe me, you'll know."

Grant focused back on Layla. "You and Chase stay
here at the cottage. We'll bring Logan back for questioning, and then we may need your help."

She didn't blink at the dominance in the male's voice.
"Make sure they have enough staff, Grant. I can't have

the surgery unmanned, especially if I'm confined here for the time being."

Grant nodded and quickly escorted Faye out the door and on their way.

While half-aware that Chase led her downstairs to the kitchen, Layla's mind whirred with possibilities. Even if it ended up not being her sister, once the whole situation with Logan was settled, Layla was going to ask Faye and Grant to help her find out what had happened to Yasmin.

For too long, she'd merely accepted that her sister was gone, which had become all the easier once she'd been made head doctor with barely enough time to eat and sleep.

But no more. One way or the other, Layla would find Yasmin. Or, a small voice said inside her head, what had become of her.

Chase placed a cup of tea in front of her and then sat in a chair to her right. "What are you thinking?"

"Just that I've let my job absorb far too much of myself."

He nudged his knee against her thigh. "I'm going to need more than that cryptic statement, lass."

Without thought or hesitation, she answered. "I should've looked deeper into my sister's silence before this."

His leg moved and stayed next to hers. "We all have things we wish we would've done. Hell, if I'd been clever enough to figure out sooner how little my dad was doing to help the family outside of work, I would've contributed and taken care of my mother long before he abandoned us. However, if we always dwell on what-if, then we can't make the most of the present."

She sipped her tea before glancing at him, needing a distraction until Faye and Grant arrived. Maybe it was pushing Chase too far too quickly, but her gut said he wanted to finally tell the truth to someone outside his family. So Layla asked, "Were there any signs he would leave you before that night?"

Chase ran a hand through his short, blond hair. "I don't know. Once I moved out of my parents' house to start my apprenticeship at sixteen, I didn't visit or talk with my mum as much as I should have. If I had, then maybe I would've sensed my mother's worry earlier."

She lightly touched his bicep. "You can't blame yourself for that. I'm not saying you're young to dismiss you, but you are. We all become a wee bit self-absorbed at the first taste of freedom. Even I acted that way, right before I went to medical school."

He looked at her and smiled. "Now, I wondered what pre-doctor Layla was up to during those times."

Snorting, she waved a hand in dismissal. "Nothing compared to most, I'm sure. But missing dinners with my family, or not calling back every time my parents rung me, was fairly common." She moved her hand from his bicep to his thigh under the table. "But the point is, we all do something, at some time, that we wish we would could go back and change. And even if you had called or visited, you still may have never noticed. Your mother is rather good at keeping to herself."

Chase covered her hand on his thigh with his own. "Aye, maybe. And in the end, I think my father abandoning the clan was the best for my mum, no matter how painful it was in the beginning. She deserves so much better than a one-sided love." He searched her gaze. "But I do what I can to make up for it now with her, just like you should try the same with your sister. Once this business with Logan is settled, and if it turns out it's not Yasmin, then I'll help you find a way to contact her."

For so many years, Layla had relied on herself. Sure, she sometimes needed her staff or the approval of the clan leader. However, she had shouldered every extra burden given to her without complaint. She was head doctor, and it was her responsibility to ensure the clan remained whole and healthy.

But did she really need to micromanage everything? No. Accepting Chase's help with her sister would be the first step toward the new her. "Thank you."

"No need to thank me, Layla. I know it's not official, and it's still early, but a mate does whatever he or she can to help their partner. To do less is unthinkable for me."

As they stared at one another, her dragon spoke up. *Finally. If nothing else, Chase helping you to realize it's okay to accept help makes me want to kiss him.*

No, don't even think of starting the mate-claim frenzy right now. Too much is going on.

Not now, but someday?

She paused, looking at Chase from under her eyelashes. Aye, he was handsome, and fit, and clever. But she was starting to think he might be the key person she needed to not work herself to death. For whatever reason, he saw her merely as a female and wasn't cowed by her position so far.

And he made her smile and laugh. No one else, apart from maybe old Archie or Cal, could do that.

Layla replied to her beast, *Maybe.*

She finally spoke aloud again, wanting to tease him. "So if I made a list of unusual tasks, sort of like quests, you'd do each and every one?"

He leaned close, his voice dropping an octave. "That depends on the reward, lass. If it's you tied up in a bow, naked on the bed, I'd do anything."

The temperature hiked up several degrees. "Then I'll keep that in mind. You merely seeing me tied in a bow is a fairly easy reward to give."

"Not just naked, but at my mercy, too."

She bit her lip as the image of Chase's head between her thighs, licking her to orgasm, flashed into her head.

If she wasn't careful, her years of celibacy were going to make things difficult going forward.

Her dragon huffed. *You're only now figuring this out?*

He traced her jaw before adding, "But truth be told, I'll probably have a few favors owed to you soon enough. After all, you'll soon have to put up with my sister-in-law in labor. And believe me, that is worth at least ten favors from me. Faye isn't one to keep her thoughts to herself."

She couldn't help but chuckle. "Faye's not that bad. A bit spirited, aye, but she has a huge heart."

He lightly brushed the back of her hand under the table with his thumb, the action sending a tendril of warmth through her body. "She does, but she also likes to throw knives, which makes her a wee bit dangerous. So remember to keep anything sharp hidden during the delivery, aye?"

As they grinned at one another, a small weight lifted from Layla's shoulders. She had a feeling Chase would always be able to make her smile.

The only question was whether he would want to keep trying when she couldn't see him for a few days when the clan suffered an attack or epidemic. Or, if a nurse or her doctor in training fell sick and she had to work sixteen-or-twenty-hour days, four days in a row.

Chase opened his mouth as if to ask a question, but the front door opened and voices trickled down the hall.

Faye, Grant, and Logan had returned.

Pushing aside thoughts of herself, she stood and turned toward the door. Chase was instantly at her side and murmured, "Not yet, lass. Faye or Grant will come get us when it's time."

Muttering a curse, Layla paced the kitchen. "I just want to know what's going on. I hate mystery and the unknown."

"Aye, that's probably part of the reason you became a doctor." He put out a hand, palm up. "Come here."

She stopped pacing. "Why?"

"Just come here."

Too tired and wound up, she obeyed. As soon as she was close enough, Chase pulled her against his chest and held her tight.

For a second, she froze. The instinct to appear invincible and in charge coursed through her.

Then he whispered, "It's just you and me, Layla. No one else can see you."

Between his words and the comforting heat of his body, she leaned into him and closed her eyes. For a few beats, she forgot about everything but his heat, his spicy male scent, and the gentle caress of his hands on her back.

Letting out a sigh, she drew support and strength from Chase's lean, hard body. He really was fitter than she'd realized. She wondered if he did a lot of flying in his spare time.

A chuckle reverberated under her ear against his chest. She must've asked her question out loud.

Chase replied, "I do like to fly. But not just because my dragon asks for it, either. Sometime I'll show you some bonny sights nearby, ones not many humans or dragons visit. Then we can listen to the wind whisper through the heather and hills as they make a calming sort of melody."

Opening her eyes, she traced a shape on the shirt covering his chest. "I'd like that. I don't get to fly enough."

Her dragon grunted. *Exactly.*

Chase stroked her back as he laid his cheek against the top of her head. "Then it's a date. The next time we have some free time, we'll go flying. I can show you some of the bonniest places in Scotland, too. I've found most of them over the last few years. Of course, they'll be even bonnier if you're with me."

She tried to muster a scolding as she pulled up to look at his face, but couldn't. "Your charm is going to get me into trouble eventually, isn't it?"

He winked. "Without a doubt." He searched her gaze again. "So you'll go with me then? Once we have some free time?"

Layla of even a week ago would've protested at scheduling a date with anyone. And now, a part of her hungered to have more of this, the two of them alone, acting as merely a male and female. No work, no clan, no major responsibilities.

Not that she completely forgot about what was happening upstairs with Logan, but it wasn't as all-consuming as it had been ten minutes ago.

She nodded, and Chase pulled her back against his chest. They stood like that, silent and holding each other, for a long time. She wondered if she could do this often, whenever she felt like it.

Her dragon murmured, *If you accept him as our mate, then aye.*

It's too soon.

Her beast fell silent, and Layla merely enjoyed the male in her arms for as long as she could. Even without words, the moments were some of the best in recent memory.

Only when the door to the kitchen opened did Layla raise her head and step away from Chase. Faye stood nearby, looking between them. "Once this is sorted, we're going to talk about you two. But for now, Logan wants to see you, Layla."

Chase moved to follow her, but Faye shook her head. "You stay here with me, little brother. Layla will be fine on her own for a few minutes."

Layla noticed Chase's pupils flash, but he eventually nodded. "Aye, of course she can. But if you need me, Layla, just ask."

She had no idea how she deserved such a caring,

determined male. But now wasn't the time to think about it. "I will." Wanting to lighten the mood a bit. "Just make sure to watch the knives whilst you're with Faye."

Faye growled, but Layla turned before the younger female could say anything.

It was time to find out what was going on with Logan.

Chapter Eight

C hase had never seen someone who clearly craved affection as much as Layla did and resist it so bloody much. Almost as if being held was a weakness.

As he'd held her against his chest for several minutes, a sense of protectiveness and tenderness had bloomed. He'd never been more certain that waiting for Layla had been worth it. Not all true mate pairings were the best for both parties, but he liked to believe it was in their case. Because if anyone could find a way to sneak off and show Layla a good time without attracting much notice, Chase was it.

As time had ticked by, with Layla's softer form heavy against him, he'd imagined seeing her every day, both in and out of bed, and smiled. If he'd thought he'd wanted her before, he'd been naïve. He wanted to be the one to protect her, comfort her, and simply make her laugh.

Layla MacFie would be his, end of story.

All too soon, their private moment ended and Faye

had barged in. The fact Layla hadn't tried to instantly push him away spoke volumes about how she was warming up to him.

Once Layla left to talk to Logan, Faye searched his gaze and asked, "Are you sure you can handle what's to come, Chase?"

Seeing as Faye had been his brother's mate for more than half a year, her attempts at dominance didn't faze him. "If you mean the life of a doctor's mate, then aye, I can handle it."

Faye shook her head, her brown curls bouncing. "Not just that. I want Layla to be as happy as anyone else, but it's unheard of for a younger dragon-shifter male to take an older female as a mate. Everyone will tease you both, as well as try to pressure you to take a younger female, if only to help our race survive."

Anger gathered in the pit of his stomach. "This isn't the fifteenth century when we were barely surviving extinction, Faye, and you bloody well know it. Fuck, just your family alone is going to repopulate our clan."

As Faye placed a hand over her belly, her lips curled upward. "Aye, and one day the MacKenzies will take over everything, I'm sure. But I'm just trying to prepare you, Chase. You're my younger brother now and I don't want you to get hurt."

He clenched his fingers into fists. "Everyone judges me by my age, but it's just a number. There are males twice my age who are bloody hopeless at anything. Not to mention I've controlled myself for two years—two long years—knowing the whole time that Layla is my true mate and I couldn't have her. I won't force anything on her, but I'm sure as hell going to try my best to win her over."

Faye grinned and bobbed her head. "Good, you've passed the test. I needed to make sure you were serious. Layla isn't the type to let people in easily, and I couldn't stand to see her heartbroken if you decided to give up when things turned difficult."

He growled. "Be grateful you're pregnant, Faye. Otherwise, I'd be tempted to challenge you to some sort of competition. Not flying, of course, but something else."

Faye's face softened, no doubt because he was considerate of her wing, which had been damaged a while ago by a group of Dragon Knights, and had never been quite the same since. She finally muttered, "Even if I weren't pregnant, it's not like I could accept the challenge anyway. I promised Grant not to do anything overly dangerous because of the bairn—both now and after the wee one is born."

He snorted. "We'll see how long that lasts."

Faye put out a hand. "So are we okay then? You're a fine male, Chase, don't doubt that for a minute. But I like to meddle a wee bit here and there, as you well know. I can't help it."

The fact Faye even admitted she liked to meddle was a big concession.

With a sigh, he took Faye's hand and shook. "Aye, you're forgiven. Although if you plan to test Layla in your own way, wait a while, okay? It's taken me months to get her to even look at me. Let me charm her a bit more before you regale her with all my faults."

Before Faye could reply, her mobile beeped. After quickly checking the message, she opened the door. "Come on. This conversation will have to wait until later. Right now, Grant and Layla want us upstairs."

With a nod, Chase followed his sister-in-law upstairs.

ONCE INSIDE THE room with Logan, Layla had allowed Grant to do the talking, waiting for him to ask the most important question—why was Logan stealing supplies?

Of course, as the minutes ticked by, she began to tap her foot a little against the ground.

Her dragon huffed. *Grant wastes so much time asking about little things, such as what was stolen and for how long. He should've asked these before we came.*

I'm sure there's a reason or process. Grant knows more about interrogation and confessions than we do.

Her dragon grunted and fell quiet.

Layla kept willing Logan to look at her, but he didn't. The behavior was different from his usual bold, outgoing personality.

Maybe it was shame, or maybe even something else, she didn't know. But all Layla knew was that she didn't like how Logan acted as if he were a stranger.

Finally, Grant asked the question Layla longed to hear. "Who did you give the supplies to?"

Logan hesitated before answering, "I need a guarantee first."

Grant raised an eyebrow. "You're not in a position to negotiate, lad."

Logan continued as if Grant hadn't spoken. "I want you to promise to hear out a few people before simply handing them over to the DDA."

The DDA, or Department of Dragon Affairs, was the human government oversight department that determined how dragon-shifters lived inside the UK. Logan's request meant that at least one person involved had to be a dragon-shifter. True, it could be a dragon hunter or Dragon Knight—enemies of the dragons who broke laws left and right—but she doubted it.

Or, at least, her heart didn't want to believe Logan was trying to protect one of them.

Grant took his time replying. "I've never simply handed someone over to the DDA without first talking with them myself, not even when it's a fucking hunter."

Logan nodded, seeming to trust Grant's words. He took a deep breath and stated, "It was for my brother and…"

"And who else?" Grant prompted.

Logan's eyes finally met Layla's. "Yasmin and her unborn child."

Layla's heart skipped a beat. "What?"

Logan's gaze turned apologetic. "It's true, Layla. My brother and your sister were in love when Yasmin had been sent away. Apparently, Phillip went after your sister, snuck her away from Clan One in Iran, and they've been on the run ever since."

She tried to make her mouth work, but no words came out. While she'd known her sister had fancied a lad from Lochguard, Yasmin had said nothing about love.

And certainly not that she'd loved Phillip Lamont, the male who'd made Yasmin's life hell growing up.

Shaking her head, Layla said, "I don't understand. Phillip hated my sister and went out of his way to embarrass her."

Logan shrugged. "I can't claim to know all the particulars, but something she said one day, in secondary school, changed how he viewed her. He stopped teasing her in public, but I never suspected he fell in love with her. Trust me, I had no bloody idea he'd run after Yasmin when he disappeared, or I would've said something to the clan leader."

A multitude of questions swirled in her head. Why had her sister run? Where had they been for the past five years? Why had they come back now?

However, before she could make her voice work, Grant turned to her and asked, "Can I bring Faye in here, Layla? The fewer times we have to explain everything, the more time we can focus on solutions."

His question snapped her back to the situation at hand. "Aye, but have her bring Chase, too. He deserves to know what's going on since he helped me figure out it was Logan in the first place."

She expected Grant to go on about security and clearances, but he merely nodded and took out his phone. After putting it away again, he focused back on Logan. "Tell me plainly—are they in danger?"

"Possibly," Logan stated. "You'll see why after I explain everything."

Layla nearly leaned across the table and growled for

him to tell her why. After all this time, would Layla only find her sister to lose her again?

However, Faye and Chase burst through the door before she could do it. Without thinking, she instantly sought out Chase's gaze. Before she could blink, Chase sat in the chair beside her. Questions burned in his gaze, but he remained quiet. He merely put his hand face up on his thigh in invitation. She didn't hesitate to put her hand in his, and he instantly curled his fingers around her chilled ones.

While still afraid of what Logan could say about her sister, Chase's firm grip gave her a wee bit more strength to face it.

Thankfully she didn't have time to dwell on that tidbit because Grant spoke up again. "Now, tell us what's going on with Phillip Lamont and Yasmin MacFie."

Faye drew in a breath, and Grant quickly added. "Aye, they're together and nearby. Yasmin is expecting a bairn, too." Grant returned his brown-eyed stare to Logan. "Start talking."

Logan didn't hesitate. "The day before Yasmin was due to mate the Iranian bloke, my brother found a way to talk to her and convince her to elope with him. The Iranian clan put a price on her head and anyone who might've taken her. From what Phillip says, it's considered an act of war to steal an intended mate away once an agreement has been reached."

Faye growled. "What century is this?"

Grant put a hand on Faye's shoulder and squeezed. "It's tradition, love. I'm sure there's a reason for it. Maybe they had long-standing troubles with people stealing mates, aye? Don't judge without all the facts."

Faye didn't look mollified one bit, but Layla was grateful that Logan spoke again since she hungered for more information. Logan said, "Regardless, they were afraid to come back here since it could bring trouble to Lochguard. My brother made me swear not to tell anyone or they'd run again."

Layla found her voice. "They came back because of the bairn, didn't they?"

Logan nodded. "Aye, they did—they've been back for nearly a month. Your sister hasn't been faring well the last few weeks, and I stole supplies to try to help her."

Not caring that she should've deferred to the co-head Protectors since it was their interrogation, Layla raised her voice. "You should've come to me, Logan. You're a good nurse, maybe the best I have, but I'm still the doctor. I can help her more than you can." She released Chase's hand and stood. "I need to see my sister. Now. Tell me where they are right this minute so I can help them."

Logan shook his head, his voice weary as he replied, "I promised I wouldn't share their location, Layla. As soon as you finish your visit and leave, they'll run. They've both brought so much trouble to our families already, and they refuse to bring more, no matter how many times I've tried telling them that all we want is for them to be safe."

She wasn't entirely sure her parents would agree. They might even try to contact the Iranian clan, or maybe disown Yasmin for her betrayal. At those thoughts, she clenched her fingers into fists, anger too tame a word for how she'd feel then.

However, she couldn't only blame her parents. Layla hadn't fought hard enough for her sister in the past—especially when it came to contacting her and ensuring she was well—but that was going to change. Layla just needed Logan to bloody tell her where Yasmin and Phillip were.

In that moment, all the years they'd worked together vanished, and Layla wanted nothing more than to put a talon to his throat and demand the truth.

She barely noticed Chase stand beside her. He spoke firmly, "Then tell me where they are, Logan. My best guess is that you're not supposed to tell Finn, Layla, the Protectors or any family. But I'm fairly sure they didn't include a young, brilliant, charming electrician in that list. Or, failing that, that you couldn't tell a human their location. I'll fetch one of the human females right now if need be."

Logan's pupils flashed, and after one long minute, he muttered, "They didn't mention you or the humans specifically."

Chase grunted. "Aye, well, then tell me where they are. The others are here merely by chance."

For a split second, all Layla could do was stare at Chase. Even without asking, he had her back.

She had a feeling he'd always have her back.

In the next beat, Logan looked at Faye and Grant. His voice interrupted Layla's thoughts. "First, promise me that you won't immediately turn them over to the DDA or let the clan know they're back."

Faye spoke. "We'll have to tell Finn and our most trusted Protectors to go with you, but I don't see why we couldn't wait to tell anyone else for a wee while, at least." She looked at Grant. "Right?" Her mate grunted his agreement, and she looked back to Logan. "You have our word. Now, tell Chase where they are."

Logan looked at Chase. "They're in the abandoned cottage in the nearby woods, where the old game hunter used to live."

Like everyone on Lochguard, Layla knew where it was. "And tell me everything I need to know about my sister's health, and quickly."

"Her blood pressure's high, she started having a fever late last night, and I'm worried her dragon might take over and do harm to the bairn before he or she's ready to come."

Layla muttered a curse. If a female tried to shift into a dragon during the last few weeks of pregnancy, it could trigger contractions. And any child born while a female was in dragon form usually died since the bairn couldn't shift until they were older, and a dragon's vaginal muscles were too strong for a child in human form.

Trying not to think of her sister's dragon inadvertently crushing the bairn to death, Layla moved to the door. "Anything else?" Logan listed off a few medications he'd administered. Once he finished, Layla motioned at Chase. "Come, I'm going to need your help carrying things from the surgery."

And your support, too, she thought to herself, doing her best not to run down the stairs and fall before dashing into the night.

Chapter Nine

Over the years, Layla had learned how to compartmentalize her life into two sections—one for her role as a doctor and the second for everything else. The ability was so ingrained that she easily packed away the fears, joy, and anger rolling inside her as she made her way toward the abandoned cottage in the forest where her sister should be.

Aye, she'd have words with her sister eventually. But first, she needed to ensure Yasmin was healthy and not in any immediate danger, meaning only her doctor's side could show right now.

Her dragon spoke up. *If things were really dire, Logan would've let us know. So we don't really need to worry just yet anyway.*

That seems a bit too easy. I need to be ready in case her condition worsens, or her bairn goes into distress.

Which could easily happen because of overwhelming stress. And since Logan's hesitation to share their location had been obvious, almost as if he truly believed he'd lose his brother again if he said something, stress was definitely a major concern.

Her beast huffed. *If nothing else, emphasize protecting the bairn. Their dragons won't be able to ignore that.*

Since dragon halves valued children above almost anything else, her beast was correct. *Maybe. However, if Yas isn't doing well, the last thing we need to do is worry her further. I'll do whatever's necessary to keep both her and her bairn healthy, and if that means knocking her unconscious if she protests, I'll do it.*

They reached the hill and she paused a beat. The cottage would be just at the top of it.

After nearly five years, she was moments away from seeing Yasmin again. The sister who had once been her greatest supporter of Layla's career choice, standing by her no matter what others said about female doctors being weaker.

Yasmin. Would she be the same? Or, appear a stranger? Layla had no idea.

Since her dragon had slightly crumbled the divide between her doctor's side and her true self, emotion choked her throat. *See what you did? I need to focus on being a doctor right now, and nothing else. Don't weaken the walls again whilst we're here.*

Her dragon curled into a ball and laid her head on her front paws, the usual position she took when Layla had to see or operate on patients.

As Layla tried to patch up the wall as she continued walking, Chase, who'd been quiet and taking her orders without blinking, finally spoke. "I'm still waiting for you to tell me what to do once we're there, lass."

Not slowing her pace, she seized on the question and answered, "I hope it doesn't come to it, but if Phillip tries to take Yasmin and run, I need you to prevent him from doing so."

"You want me to get between a male and his pregnant mate?" he asked a bit bewildered.

She glanced at him. "Aye, can you do it?"

He sighed. "I'll try, but I hope it doesn't come to it."

"Me, too," she murmured, fully aware she was asking a lot of Chase since he wasn't a warrior, soldier, or any sort of athlete. Aye, he was fit enough, but it was always dangerous to come between a male and his pregnant mate in the best of times. "But a few of the Protectors shouldn't be far behind. You just need to help me until they arrive."

He nodded without complaint.

Maybe she'd asked too much and should've waited an extra fifteen minutes for the Protectors to be roused. If Chase were hurt, she wouldn't be able to focus, and her sister and her mate could run.

However, she couldn't have waited around with Yasmin so close, no matter what. Her rational brain was on the blink right now.

Besides, there were a few tricks they could use to help their cause. And as Layla debated trying to teach him how to restrain Phillip with drugs instead of force, Chase asked softly, "Will you be okay, Layla?"

On the surface, of course she'd be fine. Medicine was a muscle she'd honed over time and could use under any circumstance without a thought.

However, after so many years had passed without a

word, she was about to see her sister once more. Not only that, Layla could lose her again shortly after through either her running away or if there was some sort of complication during the birth.

She shouldn't be fine.

However, not wanting to crack her inner divide again, she blew out a breath and murmured, "I'll bloody well have to be."

Chase turned more toward her and reached out a hand to gently touch her shoulder. "I have faith in you, but we're still going to talk about this afterward."

Chase and his always wanting to talk about her, her feelings, and her past.

And yet, she couldn't help but smile a fraction. He pried because he cared. It'd been so long since someone had watched her so closely or dared to suggest she wasn't invincible. She knew most of the clan bloody well thought she was.

The more time she spent with Chase, the more she wondered if they would fit together in the end.

A small stone cottage with an old thatch roof that desperately needed replacing came into view. Hefting her doctor bag higher to better climb the incline, she reached the door in no time.

The urge to barge inside was strong, but she merely raised a hand and knocked. Nothing happened, so Layla raised her voice. "If you're in there, Yas, let me in. I can help."

After an indiscernible murmur, the door swung inward. The thin, wild-eyed form of Phillip Lamont greeted her. She barely noted how much older he looked than when she'd last seen him before he growled, "Logan wasn't supposed to tell you about us."

Used to dragonmen threatening her with growls and shouting, Layla merely raised her brows. "He didn't tell me. He told Chase, and I just happened to be standing there at the time. Now, let me in so I can help my sister."

Yasmin's soft voice drifted to her ears, weaker than she remembered it being. "Let them in, Phillip."

After narrowing his eyes, Phillip stepped aside and allowed her and Chase to enter.

Layla immediately noticed her sister lying on an old wooden bed frame, the mattress lumpy and not as clean as she would've liked.

Yasmin's face was pale under the tan color of her skin, her cheekbones too stark, and a protruding belly rose beneath the blanket. Her once black hair had threads of silver, and her face was lined with smile lines around her mouth and eyes.

However, the shadows under her sister's eyes immediately kicked her into action. Layla rushed to the bed and put her hand on her sister's brow. At the burning touch, she forgot about everything else but her newest patient. "Chase, bring the IV stand and bag here. Find the kit I told you about, the one with the needle to connect to the tubing."

Phillip stood on the other side of the bed. "What are you doing to her?"

"Helping her. She's had a fever for at least a day and is probably dehydrated. I want to give her fluids first before doing anything else." She finally looked at Yasmin again. "You haven't developed any allergies since you left, have you?"

Yasmin shook her head. "No, I don't think so."

In an ideal world, Layla would have Yasmin's medical history at her fingertips and could scan her yearly exams for any new information.

But she didn't have any of that. So after she inserted the needle and connected the IV drip, she murmured, "I'm going to examine you. Answer my questions as I go, aye? And don't hold anything back."

Yasmin nodded slightly as Layla placed her stethoscope on Yasmin's abdomen. Inwardly relieved at the wee one's quick, steady heartbeat, she then proceeded to touch and examine the rest of her sister's body, only pausing to tell Chase to turn around when she had to remove her sister's nightgown.

Once Yasmin was tucked back under the covers, Layla looked first at Yasmin, then at Phillip, and back again as she said in her best firm doctor voice, "Yasmin is at risk and needs the more modern equipment of my surgery. I can try to do what I can here, but without a steady source of electricity beyond that old generator outside, it will be extremely limited. And before you protest or threaten to run away, know this." She quickly retrieved a prefilled syringe, pushed out any air, and placed the needle near a vein on her sister's arm. "I can render Yas unconscious with one push if need be."

Phillip growled. "I don't like your threat."

She never flinched from the flashing eyes, full of anger and a wee bit of fear. "And I don't want my sister or your bairn to die."

117

They stared at each other for a few beats before Chase's voice filled the small space. "I know you two left under the old clan leader, but trust me, Finn Stewart is different. He'll welcome you back and do what he can to protect you. And whilst you probably don't know me, I'm unrelated to any of you and have the most objective stance. And so let me repeat—Finn will help you. So if that's your reason for hesitating, then ignore it."

Yasmin placed a hand on Layla's arm, and she instantly met her sister's gaze as she whispered, "But if Azar finds out I'm here, his clan will come after us. Anyone who helps us is in danger."

Azar Samadi was the male whom Yasmin had been arranged to mate. She didn't know much about him, to be honest. But if he still held a grudge after all these years, Layla would never be able to forgive him.

Her dragon whispered. *Worry about that later. For now, focus on Yasmin.*

Right, her sister, who looked so pale and frail.

Layla wanted nothing more than to comfort her sister, but she focused on the long term and kept the syringe where it was. Putting as much truth in her words as she could manage, Layla replied, "Finn is a good clan leader, one who's managed to get out of a lot of difficult situations over the last few years. He also has strong allies who will stand by him. So don't worry about putting us in danger, Yas. Finn will find a way to protect us all. Please, trust me on this, if nothing else."

Yasmin's pupils flashed to slits and back before she nodded. "I trust you." Her eyes moved to Phillip. "Let's try, Phillip. I'm so tired of running."

As Phillip stroked his mate's forehead and murmured soothing words, it was plain to see how much he loved Yasmin. His voice softer, Phillip finally spoke to Layla again. "Okay, we'll go. I'll carry her back to Lochguard."

Removing the needle from near Yasmin's arm, she nodded. "If you need to rest for a few minutes on the way back, just let us know."

"I won't have to rest," Phillip growled.

"Of course not," she murmured, not wishing to prickle a protective mate unnecessarily. "But let me help you arrange the IV drip once you have Yasmin in your arms. I don't want to take it out again."

And as she helped arrange her sister in Phillip's arms and then packed up her bag, Layla hoped Finn wouldn't murder her later on for speaking on his behalf.

Her dragon huffed. *Of course not. He'll always help the clan when asked, even for those who have been gone a wee while.*

Aye, I know. But I can't imagine he'll be happy with the news.

Well, it's a good thing we won't have to be the ones delivering it then. Faye and Grant will do it.

You're horrible, she replied with a half laugh inside her head.

Before she knew it, they were all making their way back toward Lochguard. And Layla did her best not to think about reunions, arguments, and everything else that would come later. For the moment, her sister was back and coming home. That was all that mattered.

FINLAY STEWART CROUCHED in front of the large, wooden

desk inside his office and watched the baby golden dragon underneath as she scurried back and forth, daring him to snatch her. Every time he tried to catch his daughter, she scurried out of reach. For a baby dragon, she was bloody fast.

Using the soothing voice that worked best on his wee rascal, he said, "Freya, love, come on. Daddy needs to do some work."

He waited until she came a little bit closer before he tried to grab her. However, she dashed right by him and ran across the room.

His inner dragon laughed, the bastard.

Normally, Finn would love nothing more than to play with his daughter for a short while. But his near-daily conference call with Clan Stonefire's leader, Bram Moore-Llewellyn, was due to start in ten minutes. And if Freya remained in the room, she would undoubtedly jump into Finn's lap and try to steal the camera time for herself. For who knew what reason, she'd taken a shine to the other dragon clan leader, which meant she'd preen and try to charm him the entire time and nothing would get done.

His mate, Arabella, always smiled smugly when Finn complained of his daughter being too charming for her own good. His mate would then mention it was only fair —a charming daughter for a charming father.

Not about to let the wee rascal win this time, Finn scanned the room and devised a way to corner and catch his daughter. He was about to make his first move when the door opened, revealing Grant McFarland and Faye

MacKenzie. At the sight of their tense jaws, he sighed. "Now what?"

Freya raced right past them into the hallway, and he heard his mate's voice say, "I have her!" before Faye and Grant walked into the room, shut the door, and Faye said, "You might want to sit down for this."

He searched his cousin's eyes. "Just tell me, Faye. Is it the hunters or Knights again?"

She shook her head, her wild hair bouncing around her face. "No. It has to do with Yasmin MacFie and Phillip Lamont."

Finn frowned as he tried to recall what he knew of the pair. "Didn't they both go missing, years before I took over the clan?"

Grant grunted. "Aye, that's them and they've returned. And before you say that's a good thing, it's quite possible that keeping them on Lochguard means one of the Iranian dragon clans will come knocking at our door. And not in a good way."

Sliding into his chair, he sighed again. "Aye, I'll sit. Now, tell me everything."

Once Faye and Grant filled him in on Yasmin and Phillip's elopement, life on the run, and even their soon-to-be-born child, Grant asked, "What do you want to do, Finn?"

He spoke to his dragon, one of the few who ever heard him truly complain. *I thought life was supposed to get easier the longer I'm in charge?*

They need our help. That's all we need to know.

Of course his dragon was correct.

Finn glanced at the time and then back to Faye and

Grant. "Aye, of course they'll stay here under our protection. Keep me apprised of everything that goes on, no matter how minor. I have a call with Bram in a matter of minutes, and I'll ask for his help just in case a group of angry dragon-shifters shows up on our doorstep soon."

Faye took a step forward. "Once that's done, maybe you can visit Yasmin and Phillip? They left under the old leader and I think meeting you will help to allay their fears."

"Considering the old bastard allowed the MacFies to all but sell off their daughter, I don't blame them." Finn studied Faye's face. "How's Layla handling it?"

He and Layla were close in age and had known each other their whole lives. However, he'd never heard her talk about her sister's disappearance, not even once. The dragonwoman took privacy to a whole new level.

Grant replied, "Shaken, but okay."

The male hesitated, but before Finn could ask him why, Faye jumped in. "Chase has been helping Layla and taking care of her. I think that helps heaps."

So, the young lad had finally made the doctor notice him.

His dragon spoke up. *I told you they were true mates.*

Aye, maybe. But I'm not going to press the issue to find out if that's the truth right now. The fact Layla is leaning on anyone is a bloody miracle. Hell, she never even let us help her unless we're basically under attack or some such shite.

Finn replied to the pair, "Good. Make sure Chase can be by her side for as long as needed. Talk to his boss if required and get him some time off, aye?"

The two had barely nodded before Finn's computer

beeped with an incoming video call. "That will be Bram. I'll visit you when I'm done, and we can talk more about the possible threat from the Iranian clan. I trust you two to smooth things over with Yasmin and Phillip, and notify their respective families as well."

The pair nodded and left. Once he was alone, Finn clicked Receive, and Bram's dark hair and blue eyes filled the screen. Bram instantly frowned. "Why do I get the feeling this won't be a nice call where we chat about our children?"

"Someday we'll get there. For the next wee while, I may need your help..."

Chapter Ten

The next twenty-four hours passed in a blur. Layla stabilized her sister, treated Phillip for dehydration and mild malnutrition, and did everything in her power to get the pair and their child out of any sort of health-related danger.

The Seahaven doctor had come as previously scheduled, and without too much direction from Layla, Dr. Daniel Keith had methodically done the rounds and seen most of the other patients for the day. When things slowed down in the evening, Layla was alone for the first time with the doctor in her office.

She was so exhausted that she merely motioned for him to give her his notes. But rather than follow her order, Dr. Keith grunted and shook his head. "No. You need to go home and rest, MacFie."

"This is my surgery, Dr. Keith. I know how to run it."

He tossed his files on her desk. "Aye, of course you

do. But these are unusual circumstances. Get some rest and I'll cover until morning."

Deep down, she wanted to say okay and go home. "I can't. My sister might need me."

"Look, I get that you care about your sister. But what use are you if you're exhausted and make a mistake? And no, I'm not singling you out. We've all made them at some point." He searched her gaze. "Be reasonable and think—what would you advise a junior doctor to do in this situation?"

Layla knew she'd tell them to rest and come back later. And yet, for her to admit she needed a break would almost seem like defeat, as if she were letting her sister down once again.

Her dragon growled. *Stop it. Even Finn relies on help from the other clan leaders. If he can do it, why can't we do the same?*

After five years, I don't want to abandon my sister again.

It's not abandoning her. Dr. Keith seems more than capable of taking care of her.

You've made that decision after one day? I want to believe he's a good doctor, but it's too early to do so.

Her beast grunted. *He's done an amazing job today, which tells you a lot, considering the feedback from the clan about his treatments.*

Layla studied the chiseled face and warm eyes of the doctor in front of her. By all accounts, he had done well with the patients, even to the point Lorna MacKenzie had praised him for how he'd treated her.

Even though Layla suspected Lorna hadn't needed to see a doctor and had only come to see Dr. Keith for herself, the dragonwoman's good word meant a lot to anyone inside the clan. Especially since Lorna remembered back when Dr. Keith had lived on Lochguard, before his father and human mother were tossed out by the former leader and their son had followed, which meant Lorna had a more well-rounded opinion of the male.

As Layla struggled to keep her eyes open, she made a decision. She couldn't help Yasmin if she passed out from exhaustion. "Fine, I'll rest until morning. And you'll ring me the second anything changes with any of the patients, understand?"

"On my honor, you have my word." He smiled slightly. "And to think that my mate says I'm the most stubborn doctor she's ever met. I'm going to have to introduce her to you just to prove she's wrong."

Standing, Layla shook her head. "I'm stubborn out of necessity, as most any dominant female dragon-shifter has to be to deal with you lot." Once she picked up her bag, she added, "Although I'd love to meet your mate one day, Dr. Keith."

"Call me Daniel. And she'll be excited to meet you, too. She's human and has wanted to come to Lochguard ever since Finn started making headlines."

The two clans had been strangers for too long. But that was more Finn's problem than hers. Layla would think of talking more with Daniel and his mate at some later time, when she wasn't about to fall asleep on her feet.

Layla gave the last few instructions, said her good-byes, and made her way out of the surgery.

It was dark outside, with only the faint glow from the

sparse streetlamps. Not that it was too much of a problem considering her keen dragon-shifter eyesight.

However, she'd barely taken a few steps away from the building when someone took her hand and a familiar male voice filled her ears, "Let me help you, lass."

Chase. A sense of relief washed over her. If it were anyone else, she'd brush off their offer. However, she was too exhausted to do it with him. She leaned against his chest and whispered, "I'm so tired."

He stroked her back. "I know, love. I know."

In the next second, Chase gently lifted her into his arms, and Layla could do nothing but loop her arms around his neck and lean into his hard, warm body. His steady heartbeat lulled her into sleep within minutes.

IT HAD BEEN a lot fucking harder than Chase had imagined to simply stay away from Layla and let her do her work.

But he wasn't a doctor or nurse, and all he would've done was slow her down or worse, caused her to make a mistake. Instead, Chase had run as many errands to help the surgery as he could and did his best to give an account to Grant of all that was said with Phillip and Yasmin.

Soon he'd had nothing to do but wait.

So he'd ensured there was food to warm up in Layla's fridge and did his best to get things ready for when she came home, so she wouldn't have to expend much effort to go to sleep.

And sometime during the blur of activities, Finn had given him a strange order—to make watching over and taking care of Layla his top priority.

As if he wasn't going to bloody do that anyway.

His dragon huffed. *Finn knows Layla keeps everyone distant. You can't fault him for wanting to encourage any sort of closeness.*

I guess this means he supports the match.

If not, he would've said so.

Chase grunted. *Although it's not Finn we have to ultimately convince.*

His dragon stood a little taller. *She'll say yes soon enough.*

A companionable silence fell between him and his beast as they waited outside the surgery. As the hour grew late, he wondered if Layla would force herself to work until morning.

He'd give her another half hour before checking on her. Aye, he did his best to not interfere with her work, but part of Chase's job was to ensure she didn't kill herself.

However, after about ten minutes, Layla finally stumbled out.

And aye, she stumbled and he had to reach out a hand to steady her.

After offering her help, she leaned against him without a struggle, and his restless energy vanished. His only job for the foreseeable future was to take care of Layla. Nothing else mattered.

Scooping her up, she weighed almost nothing in his arms. He loved the warmth of her body against his, and he knew right then and there why he'd been destined to be Layla's true mate. She would never look after herself and would always want to look after others. Ensuring her well-being would be his job. For the first time in his life, he would be responsible for someone else, instead of others trying to take care of or protect him, like his mum and brother had done.

Cuddling her sleeping form more against him, he made his way toward her house, doing his best to ignore how her scent invaded his nose. Or how the softness of her breasts against his chest sent heat through his body.

His dragon growled. *How much longer must we wait? I want her.*

Not now, dragon. There's too much going on.

I know we can't kiss her yet. But there's a hell of a lot we can do without crossing that line. And it would relax Layla, too.

Maybe you want to accost the unconscious, but I don't.

His beast growled. *Of course I wouldn't do that. But once she wakes up, worshiping her body a wee bit may give her a new type of energy.*

As his dragon flashed images of them suckling Layla's breast, licking between her thighs, and watching her face as she orgasmed, Chase gritted his teeth. *Stop it. If we can't prove how we can be a supportive mate, she'll never let us do any of that.*

Supportive, yes. But I doubt Layla wants a passive one.

Not wanting to deal with his dragon and argue again, he constructed a mental maze and tossed the beast inside. While his dragon banged against the walls, they held.

Chase hated doing it, but he wanted to savor every second of Layla in his arms and not waste time debating how to win Layla with his inner beast.

He focused on the female in his arms. Even in the dim lighting, he could see her partly opened lips, her dark eyelashes against her skin, and strands of hair falling down her cheek.

He didn't think she could be more beautiful.

And one day, she might be his.

Instinctively, he tightened his grip. No, she *would* be his.

Chase finally reached her cottage and managed to get inside without waking her up. Only when he finally laid her down on the bed did she stir. "Whaaat?" she murmured.

Smiling at the sleepy response, he gently caressed her cheek before tucking a section of hair behind her ear. "We're home, love. Once I tuck you in, I'll go downstairs and sleep on the sofa."

Layla reached a hand up and grabbed his. "Stay with me."

His heart beat double-time as he asked slowly, "Is that wise? What if you accidentally kiss me in your sleep?"

She frowned and did her best to shake her head. "I won't. Please, Chase. Stay with me."

He'd done the honorable thing and offered to sleep elsewhere. However, he wasn't going to make Layla beg for his company.

Leaning down, he kissed her cheek. "Aye, I'll hold you. Let me get you settled into bed, first."

Layla remained half-asleep the whole time as he removed her shoes and maneuvered her under the covers. Maybe he should've offered to change her clothes or remove them. But a naked Layla would be dangerous and too sweet of a temptation, so he merely kept her clothes on.

Once she was settled, he took off his own shoes and climbed in behind her. The second he laid on his side, she snuggled into his front, and he put an arm around her waist.

As he held her, the heat of her body warming his own, he closed his eyes and nuzzled her neck. "Good-night, love."

She mumbled, "Night," and was out within seconds.

Chase tightened his hold on her, trying to merely enjoy the moment and ignore his painfully hard cock between them.

It was going to be one fucking long night.

But as Layla started to snore softly, he smiled. A few days ago, Layla had done everything within her power to avoid him. And yet here she was, snoring as she snuggled against him, trusting him enough to sleep with her.

His true mate was strong and stubborn, with a hidden sense of humor he wanted to coax out more often. Not to mention, she was also vulnerable and even fragile at times. The contrast stirred something inside him. He never wanted to let her go.

He loved her.

Not that he would say so anytime soon. For the moment, he was content to hold her against his body and fall asleep with her scent in his nose.

Chapter Eleven

Layla was usually the sort of person to jump out of bed the second she was awake. Partly because of her profession, but also because mornings were her favorite time of day.

However, as she slowly opened her eyes and blinked against the faint daylight streaming in through the window, warm and toasty under the covers, she had no desire to spring from bed just yet.

Then someone nuzzled her neck and tightened his hold around her middle, and she smiled, remembering Chase had stayed the night with her.

He murmured, "Don't you dare leave me yet."

She was about to tease him when his hand stroked her lower belly. Each pass of his fingers sent more heat surging through her body, making her heart pound harder.

Her dragon sounded sleepy as she said, *Move his hand*

lower. After so long without a male's touch, it won't take long to come.

Grateful Chase couldn't see her cheeks turn red, she replied, *Why would you think of something like that right now? While I know someone would've alerted me to any changes for Yasmin, which means she should be the same or better, I don't have time for selfish things like orgasms. We should get up and go back to check on her.*

Her beast growled. *You're stressed, I haven't had sex for years, and we're both ticking time bombs. Encourage him. A half hour to ourselves will benefit everyone in the long run.*

At the rebuke in her dragon's voice, Layla paused to consider the words. For dragon-shifters, sex was an essential part of maintaining their overall mental health. If any of her staff had been as strung tight or overworked as she was, Layla would've advised them to find a willing partner and relax a wee while.

She hated when her beast was not only rational but correct.

Maybe, just maybe, she could spend a little time on herself for once, provided there wasn't some sort of emergency waiting for her on her mobile phone. It wouldn't even be entirely selfish, either. If she were more relaxed, her sister and everyone else would benefit, too.

Her dragon spoke again. *Then encourage him. He's been patient, and probably will remain so unless he knows you want his touch, too.*

As she debated what to do—Layla was bold and straightforward as a doctor but less so when it came to being a lover—Chase's hand went an inch lower. He murmured, "As your future mate, it's my job to take care of you in all ways. And before you say it's not important, just know that you were moaning my name in your sleep, lass."

Her cheeks heated even more. "Don't say that."

His fingers moved even closer to the now throbbing bundle of nerves between her thighs. "It's nothing to be embarrassed about, love. But it did mean I couldn't sleep well, and instead, I lay awake thinking of a hundred ways to make you moan in reality." His fingers stilled and Layla nearly cried out no. He added, "Let me try one of them, aye?"

Layla wanted to scream yes. She'd been ready to do so a minute ago.

And yet, with him asking permission, it made reality come crashing back. There was someone waiting for her to make an appearance at the surgery, after all. So she shook her head. "Dr. Keith will want to go home."

Chase nibbled her earlobe before licking it once, twice, three times. The throbbing between her thighs pounded harder.

He murmured, "You're to have the morning off, on both Finn and Dr. Sid's orders."

"Dr. Sid?" she echoed.

"Aye, she's come up from Stonefire. Something about everyone wanting to coo over her and Gregor's son, and how she wouldn't turn down willing babysitters. Finn texted me during the night, as did Dr. Sid. They told me I was to enforce the order, too. And not to worry, your sister and her mate are doing better."

"But—"

He licked her neck before his hot breath caressed her

skin, making her shiver. "If you try to set foot in the surgery before 2:00 p.m. today, Dr. Sid said she'd toss you out on your arse as many times as it takes." He smiled against her skin. "Although I admit, that would be a sight to see."

She gently elbowed his ribs behind her. "Not funny, Chase."

His hand stroked her abdomen again. "The serious, proper doctor being tossed out repeatedly? Aye, it would be. Although I'll admit, it would be hard not to kiss away the adorable frown you'd no doubt have between your brows." He bit her neck before soothing the slight sting with his tongue, and she barely contained a groan in her throat. He murmured, "However, I'm willing to sacrifice seeing that sight if it means I can have you naked and squirming at my touch."

His fingers finally reached her clitoris, and as he rubbed gently through her trousers, Layla cried out and jerked at the touch.

Her dragon growled. *You trust Dr. Sid. Let him fuck us with his tongue. It will be so much better than trying to fight how randy we are.*

Layla tried to think of a reason why she shouldn't. But as Chase continued the delicious friction, the urges she'd long suppressed burst through.

Longing, wanting, lust. She wanted the male next to her touching her, licking her, and making her forget about everything but his touch.

Moving her hips in time to his motions, she turned her head and kissed the underside of his jaw. She whispered, "Okay."

With a growl, Chase had her on her back, and he was above her, his eyes full of desire. The look, combined with the way he held her wrists over her head, made her heart skip a beat and wetness rush between her legs.

She'd never wanted to submit to anyone. But the thought of Chase in control, teasing her, making her hot until he finally made her come, made her bold. Spreading her thighs, she lifted her chest and whispered, "I want you, Chase. Show me how much you want me, too."

With a growl, he held her wrists in place with one hand as he extended a talon on his free one. Her shirt was split down the middle in the next second, her bra gone right after, until the cool air caressed her nipples and turned them to hard points.

Retracting his talon, he drew circles around her tight bud, but never quite touching it. "You're fucking perfect, better than I ever imagined in my mind."

Before she could argue, he leaned down and took her nipple into his mouth, suckling gently, each pull making Layla spread her legs farther apart. When he moved to the other side and did the same to her throbbing peak, her skin burned hotter, and she wanted more than merely his mouth on her breast. She wanted his ferociousness between her thighs.

Her dragon grunted. *Then tell him. He can't read your mind.*

"Please, Chase." She raised her hips, wanting her trousers and pants gone, needing to feel his fingers against her skin.

Moving his hand to between her thighs, she cried out

when he stroked the material covering her swollen flesh. "Are you ready for me to eat that sweet pussy?"

She whimpered, and all she could manage was a half-hearted, "Yes."

He released her, shred her trousers and tossed the remnants to the floor. She lay completely naked before him.

"Look at me, Layla."

She tore her gaze away from the straining cock trapped in his trousers and sucked in a breath at his flashing eyes, full of heat and promise.

While she'd seen the fun and determined side, he'd never truly let his wanting show through. Until now.

And she could barely breathe.

He continued, "Watch me as I taste what I've wanted for so long."

She nodded, and he leaned down to kiss her belly, each of her thighs, before raising her hips and meeting her gaze again.

His tongue stroked her entrance and she moaned. He continued to lap, lick, and thrust, careful to never touch her clit. She moved a hand to his head, digging in her nails and tugging his hair, wanting him to move upward to where she pounded with need.

But he continued to torture her with licks and thrusts, making her body hotter, tighter, to the point she was afraid she'd shatter into a thousand pieces.

He finally murmured something she couldn't hear against her before his tongue found her tight bud and licked it in a slow, steady rhythm. Her hips bucked, but he held them in place. When he increased the pressure of his tongue, she groaned, coming so close. It was as if the male knew exactly what she liked without asking.

She gripped his hair harder, not wanting him to leave her.

Not that Chase gave any sign he would. Never easing up his delicious torture, she arched her back and moaned as he increased the pressure and pace against her clit. The pressure finally built and she cried out his name as pleasured exploded, coursing through her body with each spasm of her inner muscles.

Chase continued to lick and lap for a few more seconds before he kissed each of her inner thighs again, and then her lower belly. Laying his head on her abdomen, he took her hands in his and squeezed.

The sight of him, disheveled with flushed cheeks, made her insides flip. She still didn't know how out of all the females inside the clan, Chase McFarland wanted her.

Her dragon growled. *Don't do that. We're worth it.*

Ignoring her beast, she focused back on the male laying on her. Somehow she found the courage to ask, "So? Was it as good as you thought?"

He grinned slowly, contentment flashing in his eyes. "Better. I'll never tire of your taste, love. Never."

Maybe some females would brush the comment off as hyperbole. But something about Chase's tone rang with truth.

She'd never wanted a male inside her so much in her life.

And in that moment, Layla decided to share a secret that doctors held dear, one that they couldn't usually share without facing some sort of penalty from the clan leaders.

However, Chase was going to be her mate one day—yes, he'd more than proven he could handle staying out of the way when she needed to help someone in the surgery. And while she didn't have time for the mate-claim frenzy anytime soon, there was another way to share more of herself. A way that may encourage him to keep courting her instead of brushing her off with frustration if another attack, or epidemic, or other such event occurred, which would delay any sort of frenzy yet again.

Gently taking one of her hands from his, she brushed his hair, his brow, and then his lips. "I want more than your mouth, Chase."

He frowned. "Whilst most would call me an idiot for even mentioning this, didn't you say that you wanted to wait for the frenzy? As much as I'd love to kiss you and claim you right here and now, I think it's just the orgasm talking. You'll regret it instantly, love."

She snorted. "You're so confident of your abilities, to the point they'd make me lose all rational thought with just one orgasm?"

He growled, the vibration of his throat against her lower abdomen sending a fresh wave of heat through her body. She barely caught his next words. "Do I need to prove my skills to you again and again, until you are nothing but a pile of jelly on this bed?"

Her dragon spoke up. *Now that sounds like a perfect way to handle the morning.*

Not if we're to work later in the day.

Layla motioned for him to come up to her, and he did, not hesitating to place a protective hand on the swell of her hip. As he strummed his rough thumb against her bare skin, she wanted to roll him onto his back and take him right then and there.

He raised an eyebrow, reminding her that she wanted to tell him something. After cupping his cheek, she said, "There are a number of things dragon doctors and clan leaders know that others don't. Most secrets are kept for protection, or to prevent hasty decisions that could lead to a lifetime of misery."

He searched her gaze. "Aye, I'm sure there are. But why are you telling me this?"

She continued to stroke his face, loving his early morning stubble against her fingers. "Because I want to share one of them with you. Can you promise to keep it a secret?"

His hand rubbed her hip. "Of course."

She bit her lip for a second. She would tell him, aye, she would.

But a tiny part of her was afraid. He could say no and then know there was always a way out for him, to realize she was too much to take on as a mate.

And that frightened her. In a short amount of time, Chase had wormed his way into her life, showing her how lonely she'd been, and making her want him more than she'd wanted anything in a long time.

Her dragon growled. *He's waited two bloody years for us and has gone out of his way to prove he can support us as a doctor's mate. He won't tire of us.*

Chase leaned over to kiss her cheek, her jaw, her earlobe. "Tell me, love."

Taking a deep breath, the words spilled from her lips. "Potential true mates can have sex without triggering the frenzy as long as neither one kisses the other on the lips."

Chase's head shot back, his eyes wide as they met hers. "Say what?"

She smiled. "It's true. The risk of pregnancy is still there, which is part of the reason we never tell anyone, or rather strongly allow everyone to believe sex can start a frenzy, just like a kiss."

He frowned a little. "But wouldn't it be better for both parties to try it out beforehand?"

She shrugged one shoulder. "Maybe, maybe not. For the most part, keeping the secret gives a pair of true mates the chance to know each other without merely wanting the physical. Not to mention most people aren't restrained enough to remember not to kiss during sex." She searched his gaze. "Would you be able to?"

Chase didn't hesitate. "Aye, if I took you from behind. But is this what you want, lass? I can wait until things settle down a bit. Not because I don't want you, but because I want to prove to you that I want you as my mate, not merely as someone for a few tumbles in bed."

She moved her fingers to trace his jaw. "I know you could wait. You've shown that many times—last night, over the last few days, and even for the two years when I had no clue about us being potential true mates. But..."

Chase cupped her cheek and murmured, "But?"

She smiled shyly. "I don't want to wait. Aye, the frenzy can wait, and I'm not sure I'm quite ready for that." She moved her hand down to his chest, stroking lower. "But I want you, Chase McFarland. Desperately."

Her hand finally reached the hard outline of his erection punching against his trousers, and her mouth watered to see all of him.

"Fuck, the look in your eyes, Layla. There's no male alive who could say no to that."

She gently squeezed his cock and Chase groaned. "Then make your first claim, Chase, and show me how much better you are than what I've seen in my dreams over the last week."

With a growl, he sat up, ripped off his clothes, and lightly stroked his cock. Layla's gaze watched the motion, licking her lips at how hard and long he was.

With a groan, Chase release himself and flipped her over onto her stomach. "I'm not going to last if you keep looking at me like that." He leaned down, kissed the nape of her neck, and added, "But I need to make sure you're ready for me, love. So it's time for some more torturing with my lips and tongue."

And as he began said torture, Layla learned yet again how much patience her future mate truly had.

CHASE COULD HARDLY BELIEVE what Layla had told him. Not just that she wanted him, but that he could claim her with his cock and not set off the frenzy.

His dragon growled. *Don't think, just act.*

Layla was on her stomach before him, her lovely arse and hips wiggling in impatience.

While he'd love nothing but to raise her hips, thrust into her, and make sure she knew he wasn't going to let her go after this, he somehow tamed the urge and placed his hands on her arse. Rubbing in slow circles, her skin warming under his touch, Layla arched her hips upward.

He chuckled. "Not yet, love."

Aye, he wanted to tease her a wee bit, but it'd been over two years since he'd last had sex, and Chase wasn't sure how long he'd last without the benefit of the frenzy.

His dragon spoke up. *Let me take control. I can last longer.*

The challenge thrown down, he replied, *No fucking way. The first time is mine.*

His beast sat back, satisfaction in his gaze, knowing Chase would live up to the challenge now.

Not wanting to waste more time with his beast and ignore the willing, naked female in front of him, Chase moved one hand down to between her thighs. As he lightly stroked her pussy, Layla arched even higher.

He gently inserted his middle finger an inch, loving how drenched she was already—all for him—and then retreated. Her hips followed after him as she whimpered softly.

It was still hard for him to believe Layla was naked and begging for his cock.

He lazily fucked her pussy with his finger, soon adding a second one, and watched Layla's hips move in time with him. He lightly smacked her arse, and she grabbed the sheets with her fingers.

It seemed his lass liked that.

He smacked her again, increasing the pace of his

fingers. When she was nearly dripping down his hand, he pulled back, and Layla cried out. "No, don't stop."

Rubbing up her back until he reached her neck, he gently squeezed. "Do you want to come on my fingers or my cock?"

She hesitated, and he leaned down to kiss her lower back. He murmured, "Don't ever hold back with me, Layla. I have two years' worth of fantasies to play out, but I'm not a selfish bastard. Tell me what you want, and I'll do it. But you need to say what you want with words." He moved his lips further up her spine, kissing her along the way until his body curved over hers and he laid his chin on her shoulder. "Tell me which do you want—my fingers or my dick?"

She whispered, "Your cock. Please, Chase, I need you inside me."

If not for a lifetime of memories of how his mother's accidental pregnancy had doomed her to a life of misery, Chase probably would've risen back behind her and claimed her, over and over again, until they both shuddered in release, without another word.

However, Chase found the strength to ask, "Do you have a condom?"

"No, they've long expired. But you don't need to use one."

His dick let out a drop of precum at the idea of coming inside Layla's warm pussy, her gripping and releasing him in a way no other male would ever feel again.

But his voice was husky as he said, "I can pull out. Not a guarantee, but there's less risk."

In answer, she pressed her arse back against his cock and wiggled. "If it happens, it happens. It will one day anyway. Claim me, Chase, and make me forget about anything but you inside me."

With a growl, he nipped her shoulder and pressed his hard cock firmly against her arse. "Tell me again."

"I want you, Chase. Don't make either of us wait any longer."

He wished he could kiss her mouth, nipping and licking in slow strokes to show her how happy the words made him.

But he couldn't. So Chase kissed his way down her spine, slowly caressing her sides as he did so. Once he was kneeling between her legs again, he raised her hips and lightly smacked her arse cheek. "Keep them up."

Taking his cock in hand, he rubbed the head up and down her folds, pausing to gently smack her clit when he reached it, loving how he learned yet another kind of moan Layla made for him.

He spread her legs even wider, doing his best not to drool at the sight of her swollen, wet pussy on display for him. Only for him.

Placing his cock at her entrance, he pushed in an inch. "You're so tight, love. So tight."

Sweat ran down his face as he entered inch by slow inch. It took everything he had not to come on the spot.

No. His female deserved better.

His dragon ordered, *Last long enough for her to come, or I'll take control.*

With the threat renewed, Chase took a few deep breaths and thrust the remaining inches. Once he was fully inside her, he cursed. "You're so fucking tight, and wet, and perfect." He rubbed her shoulders. "I never want to leave."

Layla's forehead was pressed against the mattress. "Bloody hell, Chase, you're so big."

Male satisfaction coursed through him. Reaching around to her front, he gently plucked one of her nipples before moving to the tight bud between her thighs. As he applied pressure and stroked, Layla gripped the sheets tighter. He murmured, "And I can't wait to see your sweet lips around my dick one day."

She gripped her inner muscles and he hissed a breath. Layla said, "Torture me and I torture you."

He couldn't wait for when he could claim her face-to-face and watch her flush as she said such things. "Then it's time for some pleasure."

Chase pulled back and thrust slowly at first, increasing his pace as he went, careful to keep the rhythm of his fingers on her clit to match.

He did his best to rub her back, her arse, anywhere he could touch with his other hand. "Just remember, as soon as I can, I will be torturing your mouth at the same time as I claim your pussy."

"Chase, damn, I can't wait."

Her words snapped something inside him and Chase moved faster, the sound of flesh against flesh filling the room as he lost all rational thought but the need to fill Layla and claim her as his own. Maybe not with a frenzy or an official mating ceremony just yet, but right here, right now, was just as important.

Not just because she was beautiful or clever or kind.

This was the beginning of their future, the one he'd wanted for so long.

As he continued in long strokes, Layla's breathing quickened as he felt the pressure building at his base. Gritting his teeth, he tried his best to hold back. He couldn't come before her, not now.

Layla cried out, her core gripping and releasing him. The bloody wonderful pressure sent him over the edge. Chase stilled as he spilled inside her, claiming her with his seed.

After the longest orgasm of his life, he leaned over Layla, wrapped his arms around her middle, and maneuvered them on the bed, both of them on their sides.

He remained that way, his ear against her shoulder, as he tried to catch his breath.

Thinking of Layla's earlier words, about why no one revealed how potential true mates could have sex without kissing, made him chuckle.

She leaned even more into him and murmured, "What's so funny?"

One of his hands lazily roamed up her abdomen until he could play with her nipple, running his forefinger back and forth against the still hard peak. "Just that I can see why you don't tell people about the sex between true mates thing. That was bloody amazing, and if I hadn't spent two years learning patience, it might make me do something rash right now."

It was a sign of her trust in him that she snorted and didn't try to move away. "Aye, according to old, barely legible records, it caused quite the problem centuries ago. Something about destroying alliances, and turning one

Scottish clan against the other, back when Scotland had more than one dragon clan."

Lifting his head, he kissed her shoulder and murmured, "I will never tell a soul, I promise. Although since we know, maybe we can exploit the information a few more times?"

His suggestion could be taken as serious or flippant—he left it up to her.

Then she squeezed her inner muscles around his semihard dick, and blood rushed south again. "Only if I can ride you this time. I'll face away, but I want to feel you even deeper inside me."

With a groan, he maneuvered so they sat, Layla still on his now steel-hardened cock. "This is one of my fantasies, lass. For you to ride me, try to break me, and all the while I drive you crazy until you're the one falling apart in my arms."

She wiggled a wee bit. "Then I suppose I should get started."

And as Layla tortured him far worse than he did her, he had to bite her shoulder as he came to keep from turning her face and letting her know how much he already loved her with his mouth.

Chapter Twelve

A while later, as Layla lay with her head on Chase's chest, his heartbeat under her ear, she lightly played with the patch of dark blond hair on his chest and selfishly wished she could stay like this all day.

Aye, she wouldn't deny she craved more sex with him. But it was more than that. Layla was an intensely private person, mostly out of necessity because of her profession. And to be encircled in the arms of a male she trusted, one whom she could confide anything and was coming to care for, was almost unthinkable.

So much so that she feared it was a dream. One she'd wake from and wonder how she could easily forget it and return to her old way of doing things, where she attempted to do everything herself and forgot about anything she wanted.

For so many years, she'd lived without truly living. Layla didn't want to go back to that.

Her dragon spoke up in a sleepy voice. *Stop worrying.*

The slight soreness between our thighs is proof Chase and every-thing that goes with him is real. Stop pretending we can't have nice things and a happy future like so many others.

Others had fought for the right to that kind of future, like her sister had done.

Guilt instantly filled her body. Here she was, in a post-orgasmic haze, and her sister was stuck in a hospital room. She'd spent more than half an hour for herself. Layla should've dressed and tried to find out more about Yasmin's condition already.

Her dragon growled. *Dr. Sid is watching her, and she told Chase that Yasmin was doing better. Besides, we still have a few hours before we're even allowed back inside the building. Enjoy the moment now to help recharge us for later.*

Chase's voice rumbled inside his chest. "What are you thinking of, love?"

As his hand stroked her back in warming circles, she snuggled more against his side. "That this all still seems like a dream." She paused, and added, "And how I feel a wee bit guilty lying here in your arms when I should be doing something else, something useful."

He took the hand on his chest and brought it to his lips. After he kissed her palm, he replied, "This is bloody useful, lass. Everyone needs some downtime to relax, even a super doctor such as yourself. Besides, you trust Dr. Sid, aye?"

"Of course."

"Then know she'd tell you if anything was wrong."

As he continued to stroke her back, her guilt faded a fraction. Not completely, but deep down, she knew he was right.

Her dragon huffed. *Aye, he is. Any sane dragon-shifter knows that regular sex keeps us inner beasts happy, which means you'll be happier, too.*

She smiled and placed her chin on his chest, so she could meet his gaze. "My dragon seems to agree with you."

He grinned. "Then that's three against one. I like those numbers."

She lightly smacked his chest. "For now. Don't expect my dragon to always be on your side."

Chase released her hand and moved his to her face, tracing her cheek with his forefinger. "I know, but just remember that you have all of us on your side going forward, for whatever challenges you face."

His words brought some of reality crashing back, specifically one certain aspect considering her parents. "Aye, there are things I can't put off much longer."

"You mean your parents?"

She blinked in surprise. "Yes, but how did you guess that?"

He took her hand and kissed her palm again, except this time he flicked his tongue against her skin before saying, "They never came to the surgery yesterday, and you never left it. It's possible you could've talked to them on the phone, but I don't think you would, not for something this important."

She laid her cheek back on the firm, warm skin of Chase's chest. "You're right, I haven't talked with them yet. Partly out of necessity, but partly out of cowardice. But they were at least told of Yasmin's reappearance.

And part of me thinks that if they'd truly cared, they would've rushed to the surgery to see her."

The fact they hadn't made Layla think the worst—her parents would see Yasmin's return as a type of betrayal. Layla only hoped they didn't report Yasmin's whereabouts to the Iranian clan.

Her dragon sat up taller. *If they do, Finn will protect her. And probably punish our parents, too.*

Layla didn't want punishment, but asking for her parents to act like they had when she and her sister had been younger, and life had held more laughter, was fairly impossible.

Chase's voice garnered her attention. "It's their loss, Layla. I know you might not be able to recognize or admit that now, but maybe someday you can."

"Like you have," she whispered.

"Aye, although I won't claim to be completely over the loss of my father. But I'm better than I was even two years ago." Chase gently forced her face upward until she met his eyes. "Regardless, you're handling this entire situation better than I would have. If my parents had tried to send away a sister of mine to some foreign clan without any sort of love or attachment between her and the future mate, I would be bloody pissed. And unlike my brother, I'm not the silent, brooding type—they'd know exactly what I thought of the whole mess."

She traced circles on Chase's chest. "Well, I've never forgiven them, but I also understand that my mother thought she was doing the right thing. Her own mother —my grandmother—was placed in an arranged mating. If my father hadn't realized my mum was his true mate and kissed her, she probably would've accepted an arranged mating, too. It's not always easy to let go of tradition, especially when each generation loses a bit more of it."

He stroked her cheek with one finger. "I'm sure there are plenty of traditions that don't involve all but bartering away someone's happiness, right?"

Thinking of how her mother had tried to make her and her sister study the Persian language as children made her snort. "Aye, like trying to learn a language only my grandmother ever used regularly." She sobered a fraction. "It's complicated. Even more so now, considering who my sister and I chose as mates."

"Why? Are two braw Scottish males not good enough?" He kissed her brow. "I can be quite charming. Maybe I need to use some of it on your mother."

She tried hard to frown but laughed. "To be honest, I'd pay to see that. She wouldn't know what to do with it." Layla bit her lower lip before adding, "That is if she ever wants to see us."

Chase gently squeezed her waist. "Whenever you're ready to talk to them, I'll be there."

Searching his gaze, she asked, "Really?"

"Aye, of course. I'll always be there when you need me, Layla. Always."

Tears prickled her eyes and she tried to blink them away. Layla didn't usually allow her emotions to show with others. No one wanted a weepy or angry doctor.

Her dragon spoke up. *It's not just anyone—he's going to be our mate.*

At the thought of waking up every day to Chase's

grin and caresses, her tears faded. Reaching a hand up, she cupped his cheek. "I wish I could bloody kiss you right now."

"Me, too, love. Me, too."

They stared at one another for at least a minute, holding each other's gaze, both saying a lot without speaking a word.

In such a short time, Chase had come to mean so much to her. That thought should scare her. And yet, it made her heart skip a beat.

Her, Layla MacFie, with a mate to come home to, to love, and even have children with.

Something she'd never thought she'd have.

Not wanting to risk crying, she kissed his chest and said, "Come, let's shower. I'm sure me all wet and dripping is one of your fantasies, aye?"

His pupils flashed and he growled out, "In more ways than one."

Her cheeks burned at his double meaning. "You're incorrigible."

"Aye, and it's just what you need," he stated smugly.

With a laugh, she jumped out of bed and raced to the bathroom, wanting him to chase her.

And chase her he did, until he wrapped an arm around her waist and pulled her back against his chest. Nuzzling her cheek, he whispered, "We'll have a proper chase later, once things calm down a bit."

The thought of shifting into a dragon and trying to evade Chase's capture made her smile. "I'd like that."

Nipping her neck, he grunted. "Good. Because if

anyone deserves to have a little fun in their lives, it's most definitely you, Layla."

Placing her hands over his around her middle, Layla gently squeezed his warm skin. It would be so easy to fall in love with the male at her back.

Not that she had the time right now, of course. But maybe someday she could be as happy as Finn and his mate, or any of the MacKenzies.

Then a thought occurred to her that made her groan. "If we become mates, that means I'm going to have to occasionally attend a MacKenzie dinner, won't I?"

He snorted. "Aye, Faye will insist on it." Chase lowered his voice. "But don't worry, I'll protect you from any flying potatoes or bread rolls."

"And knives?"

"Knives, too, although I may need a doctor to give me some extra special attention afterward."

Turning in his arms until she could loop her hands behind his neck, she smiled. "I think that can be arranged."

"My cock, especially, may need some extra attention."

"That would be a pity if a knife hit there."

He growled. "That will never happen."

"Because your dragon is rather fond of your penis?"

Lowering his voice, he murmured, "I think there are a couple of people who are rather fond of it." His hand moved to between her thighs before he slipped a finger inside of her. "Right, lass?"

Resisting a moan as he moved in and out slowly, "Per-haps. Although how much attention you receive depends if you're a good patient or not. Being male, that might be hard for you."

Thrusting his finger in swiftly, Layla had a difficult time concentrating on his reply. "Something is hard, but not that."

He grinned and pressed his solid length against her bum, and Layla tilted her head. "I think I need to better judge if you're hard enough, don't you think?"

He chuckled before removing his fingers and positioning his cock at her entrance from behind. "As the doctor orders."

In one swift thrust, Layla was more than convinced. And for the next hour, she forgot about everything but the male who made her feel more alive than anyone else. Reality would come crashing down soon enough, but for an hour, just an hour, she could merely be a female teasing her male and enjoying life.

Chapter Thirteen

A few hours later, Layla faced reality. In fact, as she stepped through the doors of the surgery with Chase at her side, she dreaded it.

The surgery, which had been her refuge for so long, felt different. Almost as if she had a job to do but wanted to leave at the first opportunity to do something unrelated.

In other words, she wanted to be more than merely a doctor—she wanted to enjoy life, too.

Her dragon huffed. *Of course you want to enjoy life outside of this building. We don't want to risk having sex here and people walking in on us. The gossip would be annoying.*

Dragon, there's more to life than having sex.

Maybe. But if you're tired of Chase already, then I'll gladly take control and wear him out for you.

No way. He's mine for now.

Her dragon snorted. *You can enjoy other activities and I can do that one. After all, it's only fair to share.*

She mentally growled. *Not yet. We'll share eventually, but he's mine for the first wee while, dragon. Can't risk the frenzy, now, can we?*

Chase whispered and interrupted the exchange, "Your dragon has you frowning quite hard, lass."

"She's being annoying," she muttered.

He grinned. "So, being a normal dragon, then, aye?"

Her beast huffed. *He wouldn't say things like that if I were in charge and riding his cock.*

Before Layla could reply, a familiar brown-haired female figure emerged from the door toward the back. Despite the fact Dr. Cassidy "Sid" Jackson had a very young bairn, she looked remarkably awake and was even smiling. All the years of running on little sleep as a doctor must've come in handy for taking care of her son.

Sid stopped a foot in front of them, glanced from Layla to Chase and back again, and nodded. "Good. You both look fairly well-rested and mostly relaxed, as I'd hoped."

Layla's gut said that Sid knew they'd slept together. It took everything Layla had to keep her head up and her cheeks from blushing. "Aye, and ready to go back to work. How's my sister?"

The other female motioned toward the rear door, the one that led to the private patient rooms. "Yasmin is awake and doing much better. She's been asking for you, so why don't you see for yourself?"

Guilt crashed down on her. Layla should've been the one to monitor her sister. Instead, she'd been home, having sex and forgetting about everything for a wee while.

Sid placed a hand on her arm and murmured, "I see the guilt on your face. Push it aside. You'll do much better work now than if you had barely nabbed an hour or two of sleep. Everyone needs a break sometimes." She paused a second before adding, "Once things settle down, we're going to have a nice long chat. Gregor has always felt guilty for leaving Lochguard in such a rush, and it's plain to see he forgot to give you some good advice before he left. Not that you haven't done a bloody good job, but there are a few things I think you need to hear, Layla."

Sid was older than Layla by a number of years and had more than proven herself as a doctor, too. Which meant Layla took her advice to heart. She bobbed her head. "Aye, we'll talk. But first, let me see Yasmin."

"Go on through. The staff knows you're allowed back inside."

She raised her brows. "You really would've thrown me out on my arse if I'd come in earlier?"

Sid also raised her brows. "Yes, I would have. Not only am I a doctor, I'm mated to one. And we're an overly stubborn lot. If it comes to a battle of who wins in the end, rest assured that it'll be me."

The Stonefire doctor had never exaggerated, at least that Layla knew of. She suspected if Sid said she'd win, she probably would.

Anxious to see her sister, Layla headed toward the back door. Chase tried to follow, but Dr. Sid took his hand to hold him back. For a split second, Layla forgot how Sid was mated and a new mother. She didn't like another female's hand on her male. She may just have growled out loud.

Chase must've noticed her jealousy because he came to her and kissed her cheek. "I waited two years for you, love. I'm not bloody going anywhere now that you're finally mine."

Maybe some would be upset at him making such a claim, but it helped to soothe both woman and beast. "This is new for me, feeling jealous. I hope it doesn't get in the way of my work."

Tracing her jaw, he murmured, "You'll adjust soon enough. After all, you're in control of all the drugs that can make our dragons silent. Not to mention also the ones that can make us unconscious. No one will try to steal your male."

Layla would never do such a thing, but she knew Chase was teasing. "Good."

He chuckled, kissed her cheek again and went back to Sid's side.

Taking a deep breath, Layla walked through the rear door, ignoring the looks no doubt being thrown her way after Chase's public display of affection. She would deal with clan gossip later. Right now, her sister was more important.

With each step, her heart pounded harder until she stood in front of the door to Yasmin's room. Taking a deep breath, she knocked lightly and entered without waiting for a word.

Inside, Yasmin sat up in her bed, pillows behind her back, and a pile of knitting supplies lying around her. Phillip Lamont sat in a chair beside her bed, his head next to her leg as he snored lightly.

Yasmin placed a finger to her lips and motioned Layla forward.

She took a few seconds to note how her sister was less pale and her cheeks had a bit more color. Not to mention the smudges under her eyes were fainter. The almost contentment in her gaze was when Layla finally released the breath she'd been holding.

Yasmin truly was doing better.

And it took every bit of training Layla possessed not to sob in relief.

Her dragon said gently, *She's well. That's all that matters.*

Since she trusted Sid's word, Layla resisted reaching for Yasmin's chart and instead stood on the side of the bed opposite where Phillip slept. Once she took her sister's hand—noticeably warmer than the day before, too—Layla kept her voice low as she asked, "Is there anything you need at all? Just tell me and I'll make sure you get it."

"I'm fine, Layla. Truly." She glanced at Phillip. "Although if there's any way you can convince him to sleep in his own bed, I would appreciate it."

Layla's lips curled upward. "I doubt I could pry him away from your side without inducing a coma."

Yasmin looked back at her. "No, don't do that. He'd never forgive me."

Silence fell for a few beats. Not the comfortable one they'd once shared as sisters and best friends. No, years of estrangement and secrets made it an awkward one.

In the end, Layla decided to be blunt. "Why did you agree to go to Iran, Yas, when you loved Phillip? To think I could've had my sister safe here for years, instead of me worrying about how unhappy you'd be in an arranged mating, makes me want to cry."

Yasmin's gaze moved to Phillip's face as she answered, "Phillip and I had a fight, and since he never actually asked me to be his mate, I thought it best to make a clean break and leave Scotland. It shattered my heart into a thousand pieces to do it, but I couldn't keep forgiving him."

"Forgiving him for what?"

Yasmin moved as if to stroke Phillips forehead, but pulled back and clenched her fingers into a fist. "It'll sound silly now, after all we've been through."

Layla squeezed her sister's hand until Yasmin met her gaze again. "Tell me, Yas."

Yasmin sighed. "Aye, well, anytime I mentioned that I loved him, his face would shutter and he'd disappear for a week without a word. The first time, I was worried. And when he came back, he pretended nothing had happened. But with each time he left when I mentioned my feelings, he hurt me deeper. I kept asking him what was wrong, but he deflected and would distract me with kisses and sex. However, it got to the point where I had to know the truth. So I cornered him in a room, locked the door, and asked him why he kept rebuffing me, telling him that neither of us would leave until he answered."

Even though Layla knew her sister loved Phillip now and they were obviously devoted to each other if they'd been on the run for five years, she wanted to corner him and ask how he could keep hurting Yasmin like that.

"Layla." At her sister's voice, she returned to the

present, and her sister continued, "It did work out in the end, so don't try to hurt him, if you please."

Somewhere in the back of her mind, she hated how polite Yasmin was being with her. However, there were more important things to address, and so she replied, "I won't. But tell me his answer to your question."

"He was afraid, simply put. His parents were devoted to each other, and in the end, that's what killed them. He was afraid the same would happen to us. You know the stories, as everyone does on Lochguard, aye?"

Layla nodded. While Phillip and Logan's parents had died long before Layla had started training to be a doctor, she'd heard the stories.

A group of humans had captured their mother. When her mate had agreed to give himself up in exchange for her freedom, the humans had ended up killing them both by draining their blood, which they'd probably sold on the black market.

Lives hadn't mattered as much as pounds and pence.

She hadn't thought of their history for a long time. While Layla didn't understand how such an event could translate to hurting someone you love, she'd long ago learned that the mind worked in mysterious ways. It was one of the reasons she preferred medicine to psychology.

She finally spoke up. "Something must've changed, aye? Or he never would've followed you."

Yasmin smiled as she stared at her mate. "When he told me he could never fully love me or it'd end up hurting me —maybe even killing me—that's when I broke it off and agreed to Mum's arranged mating. Only when I was truly gone did he realize how he'd been a fool and came after me. He watched and waited for the right moment to talk to me—difficult since I always had chaperones to interpret for me—and begged my forgiveness. Before I could answer, he asked me to be his mate and run away with him.

"I had nothing but the clothes on my back and my bag with a little money. And while Azar had been nothing but courteous to me, there was no passion or love involved. He was following his father's wishes, nothing more. And suddenly faced with a life with a male who'd be nice but reserved for decades, or finding a way to survive with a male who'd risked everything to tell me he loved me and wanted me as a mate, I chose Phillip."

"And even after all you've been through, you would've made the same choice, aye?"

Yasmin bobbed her head. "We've had quite the adventure." She placed a hand on her large belly. "But the bairn changed everything."

After a few beats, Layla asked, "Why didn't you come to me, Yasmin? You know I would've helped you."

Her sister rubbed her stomach in slow circles, keeping her gaze averted. "I heard you were made head doctor, and I knew that you'd probably lose everything you'd worked for if you helped me and Phillip. It's only a matter of time before Azar's clan comes here, demanding who knows what for restitution." Yasmin finally met her eyes again. "I didn't want to ruin your life, Layla."

"Oh, Yas." Leaning down, she engulfed her sister in a hug. Closing her eyes, she added, "I've missed you so much. And I'm hurt that you didn't realize I would do anything for you."

Yasmin tightened the hug, her voice wavering as she replied, "And that's the point, I did know that. Which was why I wanted to protect you."

Layla pulled back enough to meet Yasmin's eyes, doing her best to ignore the tears for a second. "I'm more than old enough to make my own decisions, Yasmin. Promise me you'll never hold back from asking for my help again."

A tear fell from her sister's eye. "I-I promise."

She nodded. "Good." Pulling her sister back into a hug, Layla let a few tears slide down her cheeks. "I love you, sister. And between me, Finn, and the Protectors, we'll make sure you're safe and can live here again."

They stayed like that for a few minutes, each holding the other and trying not to cry. Or, at least not cry more. It was only when a knocked sounded that Layla released Yasmin and stood up. Wiping her tears away, she cleared her throat and said, "Who is it?"

"It's Finn."

She whispered to Yasmin. "I'd trust Finn with my life. Don't be afraid of him, aye? He'll help you."

Once Yasmin nodded, Layla went to the door and opened it. Layla used her sternest doctor's voice as she stated, "You can have a few minutes, but she should rest after that."

If Finn noticed her red eyes—which of course he would, the male noticed everything—he didn't mention it. Instead, he bobbed his head. "That's about as long as I can focus anyway. My mate is using our daughter to try and heal an unstable dragonwoman. A few minutes away is about all I can manage before I need to check on wee Freya."

So Arabella was using her daughter with Aimee King. She felt a whisper of guilt at not being there for it, but then she remembered how Sid had had a silent dragon for more than twenty years. If any doctor could better understand Aimee and try to help her, it would be Sid Jackson.

Stepping aside, she allowed Finn into the room and shut the door. She walked back to her sister's bed, noting that Phillip was awake and standing protectively over his mate.

Layla motioned toward Lochguard's clan leader. "This is Lochguard's clan leader, Finn Stewart. Finn, I don't know if you remember them, but this is my sister Yasmin and her mate, Phillip Lamont."

Finn nodded at them. "Aye, I remember vaguely. They shared some classes with my cousins if I remember right." He looked at each of them before continuing, "But enough with formalities. I know some of your story, but not all. Tell me everything and then we'll think of what to do next."

Yasmin frowned. "That seems too easy."

Finn shrugged. "You lot have been away a while. If we can overcome dragon hunters, Dragon Knights, and exiled dragon-shifters hell-bent on revenge, negotiating a wee bit of diplomacy with the Iranian clan should be a piece of cake."

As Yasmin and Phillip told their story, Layla began to think things would be okay in the end. If there was a way to make things work, Finn would find it.

CHASE STOOD in his white dragon form, watching a wee golden dragon baby frolic from one bush to the other, and decided this was indeed a good way to distract him while Layla visited with her sister.

His inner beast spoke up. *Just remember that wee dragon is the clan leader's daughter.*

As if I didn't already know that.

Still, as he watched little Freya run as best as a tiny dragon could, he put aside everything that could go wrong and focused on the good. He was helping several people—Dr. Sid, Arabella, and Aimee King—but it was yet another way he could help Layla, too. Aimee was her patient, after all. And if she healed even a wee bit from this event, it would make everyone sigh with a touch of relief.

Arabella MacLeod walked up to him in her human form, the rare bit of winter sunshine highlighting the scar on her face and the healed burns on her neck. The sight reminded him of how important this was to the dragonwoman. She'd had a long recovery herself from torture and a silent beast.

She patted his side and said, "Holly and Sid will bring Aimee to the window in a few minutes. It's best if you stand on the side of the house, mostly out of sight, and only rush out if Freya tries to run away."

He could only nod. According to Arabella, Freya responded best to male dragon-shifters in their dragon forms, which was the reason he was here.

After giving a playful flick of his tail to Freya's back,

telling her to be good, Chase went into position. He could just barely make out the window in question and tried his best not to hold his breath as Aimee came into view.

She was a year older than him, but the fear and panic she always carried, combined with the deep worry lines around her eyes and mouth, made her appear older. He had originally agreed to help for Layla's sake, but as he saw the female dart her eyes around frantically, as if looking for a threat, he vowed to do whatever he could to help her himself, too.

He could tell the second she noticed Freya hopping after some kind of insect. Her face relaxed and she moved closer to the window.

Soon, Aimee looked to be talking to the females with her. And for a second, Chase wondered if Freya's presence was truly the key to the dragonwoman's recovery.

However, in the next minute, a few dragons flew overhead and roared. Glancing up, Chase tried but failed to recognize them. Add in the fact no one would dare hover over the clan leader's house and make such noise—Finn and Ara had three bairns—it told him they were strangers.

He instantly ran to Freya and scooped her up with his front paw. The instant Arabella stopped in front of him, he handed over the wee dragon.

As the sky continued to fill with unfamiliar dragons, each roaring with his or her arrival, a sense of dread filled his belly. He had no idea how word had traveled so quickly, but he suspected they were from Clan One in Iran.

Once Arabella was inside the house, Chase quickly shifted back to his human form and ran for the main security building. He needed to tell his brother what he'd seen and provide all the details he could remember.

Only then could he find Layla and watch over her. No, he couldn't do any sort of medical procedure, but he suspected Layla and her sister would both need all the support they could muster in the coming days. There was no bloody way he was going to allow Layla to face all of this on her own.

And so he ran faster, wanting to finish his duty to his brother as soon as possible so he could take care of his female.

Chapter Fourteen

S ince the surgery was mostly soundproofed, Layla first dismissed the faint roars coming from the open doorway. Sometimes the Protectors did drills, both with each other and occasionally with Protectors from Stonefire in the North of England. It wasn't completely out of the ordinary.

She'd only just gotten her sister to sleep—Phillip, too, by setting up a bed right next to Yasmin's so they could lay together—and didn't want to wake her unnecessarily.

However, the instant Sid appeared in the doorway with one of the deepest frowns she'd ever seen on the dragonwoman, both female and beast knew something was wrong. "What happened?"

"I had to sedate and move Aimee to another location, there was no choice with all the commotion."

She quickly tamped down her worry for the female. There was nothing she could do until Aimee woke up anyway. "I sense there's more to that story, Sid."

Sid motioned into the hallway. Layla complied. Once she shut the door, she turned back to the dragonwoman. "What happened?"

"Several wings of dragons appeared in the sky, roaring nonstop. It was too much for Aimee, and she crumbled to the ground in hysterics. Once she was sedated, Holly suggested we move her to stay with Cat MacAllister temporarily."

Since Cat had been visiting Aimee twice a week and trying some art therapy, it was a good choice. Aimee knew the female well enough to not completely shut herself off again.

However, as much as Aimee being safe was important, something else made her stomach heavy. Even though Layla had a feeling she knew the answer, she still asked, "Which dragons are they?"

"No one has confirmed it, but we suspect they're from Iran."

Layla looked to the closed door and straightened the sleeves of her lab coat. "They can't know. Not yet. They're both in delicate conditions and need rest, not additional stress."

"Of course. But if the mysterious dragons are from Iran, they'll have to talk to them eventually."

"Maybe it won't come to that. Finn could negotiate a truce."

"Perhaps, but you can't keep them in the dark forever, Layla. You know that."

She did, but still, the urge to protect her younger sister hit full force. After all, Layla had failed to do that for the last five years, and she vowed to never let that happen again.

Her dragon raised her head to speak, but Chase turned down the corner and skidded to a halt next to her. If the dragons were from Iran, he'd probably know by now.

One glance at her face, and he grimaced. "You've heard about the Iranian dragons."

"So it is them, then."

He took one of her hands, his touch helping to ground her a wee bit more. He nodded. "Yes, and it gets worse. A few of them changed into their human forms and are demanding to talk with Yasmin's family. So unless you want your parents to speak for her, you need to come with me to the Protector's main security building straight away."

The thought of her parents apologizing and speaking for Yasmin—a daughter they hadn't cared enough about to visit after a five-year absence—made Layla want to extend her talons and hurt someone.

And she never hurt anyone. But for once she was tempted if it meant keeping her sister safe on Lochguard.

Chase strummed her thumb on the back of her hand, and she met his gaze as he said, "You know Finn won't simply hand her over, no matter what your parents say. Yasmin's an adult and can make her own choices."

Layla let out a long breath. "I know. However, I'm not sure how level-headed I'll remain when I see my parents, especially if they try to disparage Yasmin in any way."

He stepped an inch closer, his gaze fierce. "If you can

remain calm when dozens of dragon-shifters are injured in an attack, you can do this. I can sit in if you wish." He glanced at Sid, and then back to her. "You know what future I want."

He was talking of being mates.

The rational side of her brain said it was all too soon. They should wait longer before making any sort of announcement. Especially since there hadn't been a frenzy yet, either.

Her dragon finally rose its head and said, *You were afraid of him backing away without the frenzy, and now you're using the excuse?*

She hesitated. Layla could handle her parents and the Iranian dragons if need be. And yet, having Chase by her side would make it easier. Especially if Azar Samadi held the views of his father, meaning the males had the final say in family-related matters. That much she remembered from the negotiations five years ago.

However, if she took this step, there would be no going back. A month ago, that would've scared her. But as Chase stared at her, his warm hand holding hers, she couldn't imagine being without him. So she touched his cheek and said, "Aye, you're my future mate. So of course you'll sit with me."

If Sid was surprised, she didn't show it. The dragonwoman grunted. "Then go. I'll hold down the fort here. Come find me when you have a chance. We still haven't had that chat."

"I'll bring her back myself, once the air settles a bit," Chase stated. He tugged her hand. "Come on. Everyone's waiting for us."

And so Layla MacFie, the female who always had to be strong and in control, happily let Chase lead the way for a bit. After all, she needed to save all the stubbornness and dominance she had for the upcoming meeting. Because if her parents said anything to belittle or threaten Yasmin, Layla would have to overrule them. She could, as clan doctor. Although she suspected it wouldn't be easy.

But regardless of how difficult it became, Chase would stand with her. She no longer had to fight all of her battles on her own. From now on, she and Chase would fight them together.

CHASE DID his best to hide his joy at Layla's words. *Aye, you're my future mate. So of course you'll sit with me.*

And if not for the crapton of obstacles coming her way soon enough—no, *their* way—he would stop to kiss her and tell her his feelings.

But like so many things about their relationship, all of that would have to wait.

His dragon grunted. *If anyone ever says we're too young and impulsive, I'm going to have to growl at them. Maybe even shift so I can roar into their ears.*

Many will say it, but in the end, most will accept the mating since Finn does. So don't waste the energy devising plans of retribution. We're going to need all our wits to handle the Iranian dragons.

Aye, I know. Layla will never truly be happy unless her sister's future is secure.

They arrived at the Protectors' main security building and entered. Since his brother had told him where to bring Layla, Chase went down the correct corridor until he reached the door of the largest conference room. The door was shut, and he stopped right in front of it. Since the room was soundproofed, he murmured without fear of being overheard. "Tell me how you want me to act in there. I don't want to overstep and turn into a medieval alpha male, fighting for your honor in a duel."

Despite everything, Layla smiled. "I'll see how far I can go. However, if they are old-fashioned and a bit medieval, as you put it, then you may have to speak for me and my sister. I'm the older sibling, and as my future mate, it means you outrank Phillip in this regard."

The thought of rankings based on birth order and gender made him want to frown. Chase had never been so grateful for the easygoing manner of Lochguard. He nodded. "Aye, I can step up if need be."

She quickly kissed his cheek. "Thank you."

"No thanks needed. Now, let's ensure your sister's future. Ready?"

Layla took a deep breath. "Not completely, but it'll have to do."

Judging by the brief flash of uncertainty in her eyes, he could tell she wasn't sure how things would go with her parents. "We'll face it together, along with Finn, Grant, and Faye. We'll sort it all out, you'll see."

After he kissed the back of her hand, he released it and knocked.

The door opened to reveal his brother. When Grant raised his brows in question, asking why Chase was here when Grant had told him to let her come alone, Layla answered firmly, "As my future mate, Chase has every right to accompany me. If I need to mate him right now to ensure he can attend, I will."

His bloody brother didn't so much as blink. "Your future intent is good enough for me." Grant turned halfway and asked, "Finn?"

Finn didn't move from his chair. "I recognize it and don't want to waste the chance for a good mating ceremony celebration. We'll do that later." He motioned to the empty chairs to his left. "Come in."

They did, and Chase's gaze went directly to the older couple he assumed was Layla's parents. He'd never met the MacFies in person—at least that he could remember —but the female's eyes and nose were exactly the same as Layla's. She had to be her mother.

Both the male and female stared at the table, not acknowledging their daughter.

Chase's earlier promise about not going medieval became that much harder. Layla had done nothing to receive such cruelty. And aye, parents ignoring their child for their own selfish reasons was indeed cruel in his book.

Somehow Chase made it to the other side of the table without growling or threatening the MacFies. Layla sat next to Finn, and Chase next to her. That was when he got his first glance of the Iranian dragon-shifters.

They were much younger than he'd expected—the oldest was probably no more than in his mid-thirties. They all had dark hair and various shades of brown-colored eyes. However, the one in the middle, with a light beard, Chase studied the most since the male was staring at Layla.

Under the table, he curled his fingers into a fist. The male had overheard that Layla was Chase's future mate, and yet he was almost goading him on purpose.

His dragon sighed. *Don't give in. That's what he wants.*

Thankfully, Finn's voice filled the room and garnered Chase's full attention. "Yasmin MacFie's family is here. I've waited patiently, but no more. Tell me why you were flying over my clan's lands without permission."

The male sitting in the center spoke in nearly flawless English. "My name is Azar Samadi and I've come to exchange favors to make things right."

At the male's words, Layla tensed beside him. Moving his hand under the table, he lightly placed it over her knee, letting her know he was there if she needed him.

LAYLA HAD BARELY CONTAINED the disappointment and anger at her parents ignoring her before she sat across from Azar Samadi.

Aye, he was a bit older than when she'd met him the one time, with a few gray hairs amidst the black and deeper lines around his mouth. But it was him, the male her parents had selected to be Yasmin's mate.

Azar's father was nowhere to be seen, though. In fact, all of the dragonmen on the other side of the table were young-ish. She wondered if it was by design, to make Finn and the others underestimate him.

Her dragon murmured, *Or, maybe they are here without the older ones knowing.*

Having dealt with her fair share of death over the years, Layla didn't expect everything to automatically be happy in the end. And her dragon's suggestion would be too easy.

However, a small part of her wished more than anything that matters could be settled in this one meeting, allowing Yasmin to lead a normal life again.

And once Azar said he wanted to make things right, Layla tensed and held her breath. Chase's touch on her knee helped her to breathe again. However, it did nothing to lessen the pounding of her heart.

Finn paused a second before replying, "As I understand it, someone stealing away your intended mate is quite a grievous offense. Is this true?"

Azar didn't blink an eye. "Traditionally, yes. But there is no clan law that dictates punishment. At least, not anymore. It was still in effect when Yasmin ran away."

Layla leaned forward, but Finn was the leader and was in control of the conversation. Her clan leader asked, "What do you mean not anymore? Here on Lochguard, we like straightforward. So just tell me what I need to know, aye?"

Azar shrugged. "I prefer that way, too. It's how we ended up with the splintering of dragon clans in the last few years in Iran."

"Splintering of dragon clans?" Faye MacKenzie echoed. "How do we not know about this?"

Azar glanced at Faye. "Because we're very good at keeping secrets."

Finn jumped in, which was probably good given the frown on Faye's face. Lochguard's leader grunted. "You're being vague again."

Azar shrugged. "In short, Yasmin's disappearance triggered a fight within the clan. My father wanted to go after her and force her to mate me. I told him to let her go."

Layla blinked. "Let her go?"

The corner of Azar's mouth ticked up. "Yes. As much as I was willing to mate a female to help my father's position within the clan, I have some pride. I wasn't about to force a female who'd rather run and hide than stay with me."

Layla's jaw dropped as she tried to digest the news.

Azar wouldn't forcefully try to take Yasmin away or punish her.

The Iranian male continued, "The struggle had been brewing for some time—the younger generations against the old. You live on an island, in the northern section that hasn't had nearly as many invaders and conquerors as once Persia and now Iran. One of the ways the dragon clans in the region kept their identities despite the ever-changing humans in power was through our own traditions. However, as neighboring clans in Pakistan and Turkey began modernizing their ways, the Iranians fought against the shift. They wanted to remain secluded to honor the old ways. Except this created a growing problem—a dwindling population."

Finn tilted his head. "So you didn't mate humans, either?"

Azar shook his head. "No. It's why my father and

others had to start reaching out to those who had left Iran, to determine if they could arrange matings with their children, or at least those who were pure dragon-shifter. We desperately needed to introduce new blood into the clan. Even facing trouble, my father and the others in power didn't want the taint of human blood in our midst. A ridiculous notion, I will state for the record."

His words made Layla wonder if he fancied a human female himself.

Pushing the thought aside, Layla glanced at her mother, but she still stared at the table. She burned to ask if her mother knew about all of this—including the struggles and the enforcement of old ways—before she'd sent Yasmin away.

And yet, she couldn't do it right now and risk interrupting Finn's line of questioning.

Her dragon whispered, *They will still be here after, which means no more running or avoiding them. We'll have to confront them.*

Layla agreed with her beast.

"When did the clans start splintering?" Finn inquired.

Azar didn't miss a beat. "About three or four years ago. It's mostly settled or I wouldn't be here. Those who want to cling the old ways live in the eastern half of Iran. Those of us like me, who are trying to embrace the present, live in the western half."

"So you're not here to take Yasmin back, obviously," Finn stated. "So what favor are you wanting?"

"Before I tell you, I must do something first." He glanced at Layla. "I'm sorry your sister had to be on the run for so long. I kept listening for information about her, to let her know she wasn't in any danger. However, I only learned of her whereabouts last night, when your parents sent word to my clan. No doubt they had no idea my father didn't live there anymore."

Layla couldn't contain her outburst and turned to her parents. "You did what?"

Her father finally looked at her, his eyes guarded. It was hard to remember the hard male at the other end of the table had chased her as a child and made her laugh.

Emotion choked her throat, but as Chase ran his thumb back and forth over her knee, it helped to tamp down the hurt, anger, and betrayal rolling around inside her.

Her father replied, "If we'd kept her location a secret, the contract we signed would've made us culpable, and they would've come after us. Or, at least, that's what we understood."

Any levelheadedness she had flew out the window. Standing, Layla seethed. "She is your *daughter*. Parents are supposed to protect their children, not give them up to save their own hide."

Finn put up a hand and motioned for Layla to sit. Only because she respected the male and trusted him to take care of her and the others did she follow the order.

Finn glanced at her parents. "We'll be discussing this later, trust me."

Her parents nodded weakly, and Finn looked back at Azar. "Now, with your apology out of the way, tell me what the bloody hell you want."

Azar didn't miss a beat. "An alliance."

Finn frowned. "Why?"

"I've followed the news broadcasts about the British dragon clans. You and Stonefire have done much to help the dragon-shifters in your own country. If you are as ambitious as I think you are, you'll want dragon clans all over the world to also form alliances and share information. That's the only logical next step. So I'm offering you a chance to work with me and the other likeminded dragon clan leaders in western Iran."

Strumming his fingers on the table, Finn merely stared at Azar for a few beats. Layla didn't know much about alliances and the politics of getting along with other clans. But she sensed this was important. So much so it helped her to forget a wee bit about her traitorous parents sitting not ten feet away.

Finn's fingers stilled. "I'm open to discussing it. However, you will first order your clan members to stop hovering above my bloody house and scaring my children."

"Done."

"And then once you settle into a camp nearby—we have a few pieces of land we use for farmland that should work—you can return tomorrow with any other leaders in your community, including any doctors as they should share information as much as clan leaders do, if any came with you."

"There is one doctor with us."

Finn motioned toward Layla. "Then he or she will report to Dr. MacFie when she's ready for them. You may not know, but Layla is the head doctor here now."

Azar didn't hesitate to nod. "Dr. Keshmiri will be waiting for an invitation."

"Good." Finn motioned toward Faye and Grant. "My Protectors will show you where you can set up camp. I'll be in touch tomorrow via one of them, too."

Aware that they'd been dismissed, Azar and his compatriots stood and followed Faye and Grant out of the room.

That left Layla, Chase, Finn, and Layla's parents.

She clenched her jaw, trying her best to hold her tongue in front of Finn. He would be the one to decide the fate of her parents. And it would go a lot faster if she didn't start shouting.

But oh, how she wanted to shout some more. It was the only thing she could do and not start crying at her parents' actions.

Her dragon said softly, *I know it hurts, but there are lots of people we care for and who care for us in return. Focus on Yasmin and Chase, to begin with. They're worth more of our time than our so-called parents.*

If only it were that easy. I know we're thirty-five years old and adults, but it still hurts to know they care so little about me and Yasmin.

Lochguard's leader finally stood and moved to the opposite side of the table, preventing Layla's dragon from replying. As Finn leaned over the wooden surface, he braced his hands on the table. "Scott and Almira, you owe your daughter—nay, daughters—many an apology."

Her father shook his head. "All of this was cleared before you became leader, Finn. It was approved and endorsed. We're merely following the contract we signed. There is nothing to apologize for."

Layla narrowed her eyes at her father's words, her

sadness replaced by anger. *He doesn't even feel sorry for reporting Yasmin*, she muttered to her dragon.

The growl that emerged from Finn's lips kept her beast silent.

The clan leader looked at each of her parents in turn. "There is one thing almost universally believed by all dragon-shifters, and it's this—we treasure our children. Do you really think I would look the other way at you going against that tenet?"

Her mother spoke up, her voice a bit shaky. "We did what we thought was best for Yasmin. Azar was destined to be a clan leader, and as you learned, he did become one. No male would be better able to protect their female than a leader. He was a good choice."

Finn stood up abruptly. "But what about last night? Yasmin was brought here pregnant, in a delicate state, and your first thought? To save your own arses by reporting her to the Iranian clan, knowing full well they could mete out some sort of punishment. How the bloody hell is that in her best interest?"

Layla hadn't seen Finn this upset since he'd had to exile some member of Lochguard for not wanting to follow his leadership.

Her dragon whispered, *And it's for Yasmin and our sakes. He is a good male.*

She didn't deny that. However, because he was a good one, it meant there were only two options he could give her parents and still retain the loyalty of the clan.

Have them apologize profusely and make it up to their daughters, or be exiled.

And Layla wasn't sure how she felt about the latter

option. As hurtful and selfish as they'd been, they were still her parents. In exile, they would be vulnerable and could even be captured by dragon hunters.

She didn't like or agree with their actions, but she didn't want them to die.

Finn's voice filled the room again, garnering her full attention. "I see you have no defense. Aye, well, that's probably for the best because my bullshit meter can't handle much more right now." Finn crossed his arms over his chest and narrowed his eyes. "You know I can't let this slide, Scott and Almira. I will give you a choice, though. Make every effort to show your remorse, both with words and deeds, and you'll have a trial period to remain here. Or, if you refuse, I will give you two days to put your affairs in order and you can leave the clan for good."

The blood drained from her mother's face. "We did nothing wrong."

Finn sliced the air with his hand. "I'm not going to talk in circles with you. You have your options. You'll stay in this room until you decide which path you'll choose." He looked at Layla and then Chase. "You two come with me."

Layla stared at her parents for a few beats, willing for them to look at her and show some sort of tenderness toward her.

One second ticked by, then another and another. Neither one moved their gaze toward her.

In that moment, she knew they'd never apologize. They'd rather pick exile over admitting they were wrong.

Tears threatened to fall. Her own parents cared more for their pride than her or Yasmin.

Knowing she couldn't keep it together much longer, she followed Finn out of the room. Once in the hall, Finn murmured, "Chase, the room next door is empty. Talk with Layla there. When you're both ready, come find me."

Layla was barely aware of Chase maneuvering her into the other room, and she allowed him to guide her along in a daze. But as soon as he shut the door and pulled her against his chest, she let the tears she'd been holding back fall. And before she could try to stop it, she began to sob, too.

FOR THE FIRST time in his life, Chase wished he was some sort of soldier or fighter so he could defend Layla's honor. What her parents had just done to her was one of the lowest things they could do. They'd all but disowned her, and all because of not wanting to give a fucking apology and admit they were wrong.

Chase held her close, letting her cry as much as she needed. He, of all people, understood what it was like to have a parent leave or disown you by choice. And in Layla's case, it wasn't just one parent. No, both of them had betrayed her.

He wanted to growl and curse, but instead, he murmured soothing words into Layla's ear as he rubbed her back slowly. There were so few times Layla could let her feelings show, and she deserved the chance to grieve for what was surely going to happen over the next few days.

His dragon huffed. *I would suggest they'll change their minds, but I don't think it'll happen.*

Me, neither, dragon. If anything, they're only going to dig in their heels deeper to convince themselves they did the right thing.

At least Layla will gain a mother soon. Ours would never do something like that.

No, his mum wouldn't. She had more than proved how she'd put her sons first—she'd stayed on Lochguard instead of following her mate who'd chosen exile.

If anything, mating Layla would make his mum a wee bit happier.

Although he had no idea when they'd actually have a mating ceremony because it wasn't the right time for it. Not because he didn't want it. No, but because Layla needed to sort out the grief that was sure to come, all while trying to keep her sister healthy.

However, he wasn't going to let Layla take care of everyone else and neglect herself. Mate she might not yet be, but she was his female in his heart, which made her his to protect.

Since her sobs had quieted a moment ago and she merely pressed against his chest, he murmured, "I'm here, love. Tell me what you need, and I'll do it."

She nuzzled his chest. "Just hold me for a few more minutes, Chase. I can face the world again after that, but I just need to stay here a few more minutes."

He kissed her brow. "We'll start with that, but if you think I'm not going to be watching you closely for the next wee while and spoiling you whenever I can, then you're out of your mind."

He heard the smile in her voice. "I don't know if I've ever been spoiled before. It makes me curious what you'd do."

He hugged her tighter against his chest. "That decides it, you're going to be thoroughly spoiled until you tell me to shove some of the gifts up my arse."

"But you know I would never attempt that because it would just create more work for me at the surgery."

He snorted. Even when her life had turned to shit, his female had a quick wit. "That statement makes me think people shove strange stuff up there."

"You have no idea." She raised her head and touched a hand to his cheek. "I love you."

He blinked a second. "Talking about arses made you realize you love me?"

She nodded. "In a way. It's all of it, though. The caring gesture, your ability to let me do my work when I need it, and aye, talking about strange things like shoving things up arses, to make me smile when I didn't think I could."

Running a hand up her spine, he placed a possessive hand on the back of her neck. "I fell in love with you even before we talked of arses. That should be a bit more romantic, I think."

She searched his eyes. "Say it again."

"What, arses?"

She rolled her eyes. "No, you idiot. Enough with the arses."

Moving his other hand to hers, he squeezed. "I love

everything about you, Layla, including your lovely round arse."

Her gaze fell to his lips. Every cell in his body screamed to kiss her on the mouth. But he couldn't. Not yet.

So he moved to her jaw, her ear, her neck, kissing and licking, letting her know he would do more if he could.

Layla threaded her fingers through his hair and lightly scratched his scalp, sending heat and pleasure throughout his body.

Despite his hard cock and the nearly moaning female in his arms, Chase managed to stop kissing her skin and stand up straight again. At the confusion in Layla's eyes, he said, "We can't do this here, love. You know that."

Her brows gathered and her lower lip went out a fraction. A pouting Layla was one of the most enticing things he'd ever seen. And if she ever figured that out, he'd be putty in her hands before long.

Not that he'd mind it, especially if her hands decided to caress and touch every part of him.

She tilted her head. "There's a lot we can do without the frenzy, Chase. And right now, I need you."

Her words stirred his dragon, and he said, *Then find somewhere else we can have her. She needs closeness right now, and you can't get much closer than our dick thrusting into her hot, tight pussy.*

Layla touched his jaw. "Please, Chase. I need to feel wanted right now. And I know rationally lots of people want me, care for me, and all that. But I want you, Chase. I need the man I love."

How could he deny her now? He took her hand and

motioned toward the door with his head. "I know the back way out of this building. My cottage isn't far." He leaned over and kissed her cheek. "And here's a preview of how much I want you, Layla MacFie." He guided her hand to his hard dick, punching against his trousers. "And I'll never stop wanting you, either. I love you. Now, come on. I'll prove it to you as many times as you like without starting the frenzy."

After one more kiss to her cheek, he moved as quickly and quietly as he could. And as soon as they were inside his cottage, he showed Layla a half dozen times how much he wanted her, making sure to tell her he loved her repeatedly as well. His future mate would never doubt how much he cared for her. Never.

Chapter Fifteen

The next morning, Layla walked toward Finn's cottage with Chase at her side.

Much to her embarrassment, she'd fallen asleep early the night before. And Chase being the overprotective dragonman he was, had checked in with Finn and Sid to ensure it was okay for her to rest.

They'd both said yes, and so she'd shamelessly slept the night away.

Her dragon spoke up. *We'll be better for it. Between all the crying and orgasms, we wouldn't have been able to string more than a few thoughts together.*

We weren't that tired.

Aye, we were. And stop feeling guilty for everything. Yasmin and her mate slept nearly the whole time, too. And given the news we'll have to give them after talking with Finn, they'll need their strength.

Chase squeezed her hand and she glanced at him. His day-old whiskers made him only sexier. Damn males and their ability to roll out of bed and look better than ever before.

He raised his brows. "I spot the wee furrow between your brows, lass. What's wrong?"

"Just thinking how unfair it is that you're so sexy."

He snorted. "You are far lovelier than me, Layla-love. I would think after last night, you'd have learned how much I treasure each and every inch of your body."

Willing her cheeks not to flush, she whispered, "Not here. We're nearly at Finn's place."

"I doubt he has time to set up listening devices, just to catch whatever sort of chatting goes on nearby." He leaned over. "Shall we test it out?"

She battled a smile. "Most definitely not. I know you're just trying to distract me and make me forget what's about to happen, but it won't work this time." Challenge glinted in his eyes, and she chuckled. "Stop it, Chase. I mean it. I can't keep putting this off."

He quickly kissed her nose before pulling away again. "I know, but you have to admit it's fun trying, aye?"

"I suppose. I'd say more, but I don't need to inflate your ego this early in the day."

Chase grinned. "After last night, my ego should be fine for a wee while. What was it you said?" He lowered his voice and made it a higher pitch. "You're so hard and thick, Chase. Yes, harder, faster. Damn, it's never been this good."

Her cheeks flushed. Aware Chase could distract her for quite a while, she cleared her throat and tugged his hand. "If you ever want me to say those things again, you'll behave yourself."

Chase winked, which always made her belly flip. "For now. But when we're alone, never."

Which was just the way she wanted it, of course. It was becoming harder and harder to imagine her life before Chase had finally pushed his way into it.

They reached Finn's door, raised her brows and gave Chase a look as if to say, "I mean it. Behave." Then she knocked before he could say anything else.

Her dragon snorted. *But he's so much fun. I like him. He might finally get you to relax more.*

The door opened, revealing Arabella holding one of her sons. Since he was asleep on her shoulder, Layla couldn't make out which of the identical twins it was.

Arabella motioned with her head and said, "Come in. And don't worry about this one. He sleeps through anything, literally. His sister knocked over a cabinet full of dishes, and he didn't even stir."

Layla entered. Normally she'd ask after the triplets' health, but at the moment, she couldn't think of anything but what her parents had decided. She asked, "Is Finn in his office?"

"No, he's in the kitchen. He's been on 'distract Freya duty' until you arrived. Come on."

As Layla followed the dragonwoman and watched her murmur something to her son, Layla silently hoped she didn't have triplets, too. One bairn was a handful. How Arabella managed three at the same time—and remained sane—Layla had no idea.

They entered the kitchen, and Layla spotted Finn with Freya in her blonde-haired human baby form. He bounced her as he sang some sort of children's song. He spotted her and Chase, motioned with his head for them to sit at the table, and finished up the song.

Once he finished, he tried to hand Freya over to Arabella, but the wee lass held tight. Her fingers even turned into talons, no doubt putting holes in Finn's shirt.

Arabella frowned. "I'd try to say your daddy needs to work, but we both know that doesn't matter. She'll have to stay with you, Finn. At least until your aunt comes over to help."

Finn smiled down at his daughter. "Aye, wee Freya loves her Auntie Lorna, doesn't she?"

Freya waved her free hand and made some sort of baby gurgle.

The sight made Layla smile, too. Finn and Arabella were proof that some parents loved their children more than anything. And Layla was determined to be one of them, too, once she had a bairn of her own.

Aye, well, if she ever had the chance to go through the mate-claim frenzy with Chase, that is.

Her dragon murmured, *Did you forget how babies are made? We could be pregnant already.*

Mentally sticking out her tongue at her inner beast, Layla tried to focus on Finn and what was to come.

He finally slid into the seat across from her and Chase at the kitchen table before meeting her gaze. "I promise I didn't plan on having an audience for this. But Freya's been trying to escape in her dragon form more and more, and she'll at least stay put with me."

Layla waved a hand in dismissal. "No worries. Now, you may as well just tell me what's going to happen, Finn.

There's no point in beating around the bush. They're leaving, aren't they?"

He grunted. "Aye, stubborn bastards, they are. I wish I could give them a few more chances, but I can't risk the clan questioning my leadership. Especially when things have just started to settle after the clan split into two. I hope you understand."

Since she'd cried her eyes out the night before, Layla was able to keep herself together at hearing the news. "Of course I do, Finn. When do they leave?"

As Freya tried to roll off his lap, he readjusted her and bounced her gently. "By tomorrow at the latest. I won't force anything, but if you wish to have one last meeting with them, I can arrange it."

She didn't hesitate to shake her head. "They made their views plain yesterday. My sister needs me more."

Finn studied her a second. "Do you want me to tell Yasmin and Phillip? Or, would you rather do it?"

"It should be me. I'm not sure Yasmin or her mate will shed many tears, given all they've gone through. Add in our parents reporting her whereabouts, and it's definitely safer for me to be present, in case I need to calm her down."

The news could also induce labor. The bairn was due anytime now, and stress might just make him or her come a bit early.

Finn readjusted his hold on Freya, picked up the wooden spoon on the table, and gave it to her to play with. Their leader then looked at Chase. "So it's true, you wish to mate Layla, aye?"

It was on the tip of Layla's tongue to say she was

sitting right there. However, she sensed that in the absence of a father, Finn was going to play the role.

Chase sat up a wee bit straighter. "Aye, I do. I love her. And more importantly, she's said yes."

Finn looked back at Layla. "Do you truly want it? There's no rush, lass. I know you felt pressured yesterday, but you can take more time if need be."

She glanced at Chase, and he met her gaze as he took her hand under the table. As he stroked the back of her hand and stared at her with warmth and love in his eyes, she smiled. "I do want it. However, the mating will have to wait until after my sister delivers—and probably Faye, too—but as soon as we can manage it after that, aye, I want him." She looked back at Finn. "Although it'll mean asking Stonefire a favor again. Either Sid or Gregor will have to stay here during the mate-claim frenzy."

Finn raised an eyebrow. "What about the Seahaven doctor, Dr. Keith? It would be easier for him to visit and go home each night. Their clan isn't far from here by dragonwing."

"He seems capable, but I don't know him well enough. Maybe he can help out one of the Stonefire doctors, but I'd like to work with him more before handing over full care of the clan for a couple weeks."

Finn sighed. "Aye, I suppose that's the logical way of thinking. I'll ask for Stonefire's help. And at this rate, Bram could ask for one of my kidneys and I'd have to give it to him."

Arabella snorted from near the kitchen sink. "I doubt he'd ask for one of those. He'd be afraid to absorb some of your personality into his body."

Finn grinned at his mate. "I don't know, he could use a wee bit more charm."

Arabella opened her mouth to reply, but someone crashed through the front door, and ran down the hall in record time.

Grant McFarland burst into the room, breathing heavily, fear plain in his eyes.

Layla immediately stood. "What's wrong?"

"It's Faye. She's bleeding and in pain. I think the bairn is coming."

Layla moved right to him. "Where is she?"

"In the main security building. I didn't want to move her."

She looked at Chase. "Fetch my bag from the surgery, alert them to bring the stretcher, and have Holly come meet us." She turned Grant around. "Now, tell me everything on the way."

As Layla ran toward the Protectors' building, she hoped the day wouldn't end up even worse than the day before.

No. Faye MacKenzie was young, stubborn, and strong. If anyone could pull through a difficult birth, it would be her.

Faye MacKenzie screamed as another contraction hit. It was as if her bairn had shifted into a wee dragon and was trying to claw her way out with her sharp talons.

Iris Mahajan, another female Protector, stood next to her, not even wincing as Faye crushed her hand. Even though Grant's presence would help more, she appreciated Iris's support when the others had all moved as far away from her as possible.

Once the contraction stopped, she eyed the male Protectors standing on the opposite side of the main room. "Cowards, the bloody lot of you."

And she may have just snarled afterward.

Her dragon crooned softly a second before saying, *Save your energy. The bairn needs us.*

They're so bloody weak. It's just a bit of blood.

In reality, there was more than she liked. And she grew more lightheaded with each passing moment.

Where the hell was Grant? She needed her mate here, with her. If anyone could soothe her fears, it was him.

Because, aye, Faye was afraid. Her child was early, she was bleeding, and each contraction seemed to sap what strength she did have.

She didn't want to die. Her own father had died on the day of her birth, and Faye didn't want to leave her child motherless.

Tears prickled her eyes, and her dragon stood tall in her mind. *Stop it. We're not going to die. Layla will be here soon.*

Iris spoke softly. "Aye, they're cowards. But just think, watching you survive this is going to make them think twice about teasing you in the future about how you're weaker than them. If anything, you'll be able to tease them until the day they die for flinching at a wee bit of blood and some shouting."

Female Protectors were few and far between. Leave it

to Iris to make her smile during the most frightening time of her life. "You can help me do it, too."

As they smiled at one another, Faye did her best not to count down until the next contraction she knew was coming. Although given how pain still throbbed in her lower half, counting might help better.

However, before she could decide one way or the other, Grant and Layla burst through the door. Her mate came right to her on the sofa. Iris stepped away and Grant cupped her cheek. "It'll be all right, love. Layla's here."

Seeing her mate's deep brown eyes, Faye let the tears fall. "I'm dying, Grant."

"Nonsense. Who'll help me keep the Protectors in line if you're gone? Besides, if I could do this, you can, too."

"You couldn't do this."

He shrugged. "It can't be that bad."

She knew he was trying to make her feel better by arguing. It was a game to them, one not everyone understood.

But Grant did, and that made her cry even more.

Layla spoke in a gentle yet firm voice. "Move. I need room to work, Grant. You can hold her hand if you stand by her head." As he moved to stand above her, Layla barked to the others in the room. "Clear out. Your fear is only making things worse."

Grant growled, "And Iris is in charge until further notice. She was the only one brave enough to stand with Faye, and I say that means she's earned it."

Iris nodded and cleared everyone out until it was just Faye, Grant, and Layla.

Faye focused on Grant's face above hers. "I love you, Grant. I just want you to know that."

No doubt her mate was afraid, but his eyes remained strong and stubborn. "You're not dying, woman. There's no way I'm going to survive your family without you by my side."

She smiled, but then a contraction rushed over her and she cried out as she arched her back, crushing Grant's hand with everything she had. Layla lightly pushed and touched around her stomach, which only made the pain worse. Every time she cried out, Grant tried to hide his winces.

When the contraction stopped and the pain lessened a fraction, Faye slumped on the sofa. Layla's voice filled the room. "Your bairn is breech, Faye. Normally, I'd give some time to see if we could turn the wee one around. But with the bleeding, I can't risk it. The best option is to try a C-section."

Even through the tired haze of her brain, Faye knew that wasn't good. "Then I was right, I'm going to die."

Dragon-shifters couldn't handle human anesthesia. Adults might survive a small dose, but it would kill a child. And after all the bloody morning sickness and feeling fat, Faye wasn't going to allow that to happen.

Which meant Faye would either have to be awake for the procedure or risk using a milder sedative for Layla to cut her open and hope it didn't adversely affect her or her bairn.

Every second that passed only convinced Faye she wasn't going to be around much longer. "If it comes to me or the bairn, save my babe, Layla."

Layla looked right into her face and stated, "You're not going to die, Faye. Aye, C-sections are rare for dragon-shifters, but you're young and stubborn. As long as we do it within the next half hour, you should be fine."

"Should," she murmured and closed her eyes.

Grant took her face in his hands. "Look at me, Faye."

She obeyed and drew in a breath at the fierceness she saw. Her mate threaded every bit of dominance into his voice as he said, "I will be there the whole time. And you're not going to die, Faye. I won't allow it."

Under normal circumstances, she'd tease him about not being able to control everything around him.

However, in that moment, it was exactly what she needed to hear.

She nodded. A beat later, Holly and Chase rushed into the room, followed by a pair of nurses with a stretcher.

Her unflappable sister-in-law didn't even blink an eye at the situation, and as soon as Holly was close, she smiled. "Your bairn is a wee bit early like mine were. I think you did it to get one up on your brother."

Faye smiled weakly. "Aye, well, they'll be closer in age now. It'll be easier for my child to corrupt your daughters."

Holly snorted and moved so that the other nurses could move Faye onto the stretcher.

The entire time, Grant never let go of her hand.

And as they moved her out of the Protectors' main building on a stretcher, she silently hoped all would be well. She'd been somewhat reluctant to be a mother, but now that her bairn was on the way, she wanted the chance to see them, hold them, and spoil them on occasion.

And, of course, teach him or her how to fight and win against their cousins.

She just needed to stay alive to do all of it.

With that thought, Faye slipped into darkness.

CHASE SAT NEXT to his mother on the smaller of two sofas inside the private waiting room. Across from him sat Lorna MacKenzie, surrounded on both sides by her ginger-haired twin sons.

Lorna looked unusually pale, and he'd never seen the female so quiet. Even Fraser, the more mischievous twin, sat silent, merely holding his mother's hand.

While Chase knew Layla would be doing everything she could—probably even with Dr. Sid's help—he kept looking at the door, willing her to appear to give an update.

Because with each minute that ticked by, the tenser everyone became in the room. Even his mother was sitting stiller than he'd seen before. Faye may not be her daughter by blood, but he knew she loved her as if she were.

His dragon spoke up. *Layla will come when she's ready. Give her time to work.*

I know, but can you blame me for wanting to ease everyone's nerves?

And while he was willing above all else for Faye to make it through the procedure, the entire experience only reminded him of how he could lose Layla, too, in childbirth. Faye was younger than Layla and having complications. Would it be worse for his future mate?

Before his dragon could say anything, the door opened, revealing Holly dressed in her nurse scrubs. Even though her gaze zeroed in on her mate, Fraser, she said, "Both mother and bairn are fine." She looked at Lorna and then Chase's mum, smiling as she stated, "You have a granddaughter."

The atmosphere in the room changed instantaneously. Both of the twins stood and lifted their mother, engulfing her in a hug. His own mother touched his arm and he smiled at her. "I told you they'd be fine," he murmured. "And you finally have a wee lassie in the family to love and spoil."

Fraser rushed to Holly and gave her a long, lingering kiss, no doubt reveling in the fact he still had his mate despite her giving birth to twins not long ago.

Only once he pulled away could Chase ask Holly, "Can we see them yet?"

She nodded. "For a wee while." Holly looked to her mate. "But no upsetting Faye, Fraser. For once, be nice to her."

"I'm always nice to her," Fraser muttered. However, Holly raised her brows and he sighed. "Okay, I'll hold off until she's well. But if she expects me not to tease her ever again, then she's deluded."

Lorna clicked her tongue. "Enough, Fraser. Let's go. I need another grandchild to spoil."

Chase resisted snorting. After all, Lorna already had three.

Lorna, who had always been somewhat unsure of how to act around his mum, put out a hand. "Come on, Gillian. As the grannies, we should meet the wee lassie first."

Her mother took Lorna's hand and stood. "Aye, I think so, too. It's the first female born in my family for some time. I plan to spoil her now and then."

Lorna snorted. "Only now and then? Since this is your first grandchild, I'll let you in on a secret—it's our duty to spoil them as much as possible. Then we can simply give them back to our children and they have to deal with them afterward." She lowered her voice to a loud whisper. "I look forward to the day I can fill them up on biscuits and sweets, return them, and see how they deal with the ensuing sugar high. My own family always did that, and I think it's time to pass on the tradition."

Both of Lorna's sons sighed, which only made her laugh. "That's right, lads. I suspect it'll only get worse the more you have. Keep that in mind."

The two mothers left the room first, followed by Fraser and Holly. Fergus, the other twin, stopped and clapped him on the shoulder. "You'll be next, Chase. Just wait."

Since Chase knew Fergus MacKenzie the least of his in-laws—the male could be more serious than even Chase's older brother—he merely nodded.

Fergus motioned for him to precede him. "You go on ahead. I need to fetch my mate and make sure her sister and my stepfather are okay watching both Fraser's lassies and my son by themselves for a bit."

Chase headed toward the room Holly had mentioned

204

when she'd given her first update earlier. He wanted to meet his niece, aye. But he burned to know Layla was okay, too.

The thought of her being alone for so many years, never having someone to hold her after a difficult procedure or day, only made him pick up his pace more. From today, he was starting a new tradition. As soon as she finished, he'd find somewhere private to hold her tightly and tell her how proud he was and how much he loved her.

It couldn't wipe away all the exhaustion or bad days, but it should help.

However, when he arrived at Faye's room, Layla was nowhere to be seen. He made his way to the nurse who was standing next to Faye and asked, "Where did Layla go?"

The nurse replied while jotting something on a clipboard. "Her sister went into labor, so she should be in Yasmin's room."

He blinked. "What?"

He tried to dash out the door, but his mum grabbed his bicep. "You can't do anything to help her right now, lad. You know that. So say hello to your niece, Isla. It's better than fretting somewhere by yourself and getting yourself worked up."

His dragon grunted. *She's right. And this is how it'll always be, too. So you'd better learn how to deal with it.*

I'm trying, dragon. But I hate being so useless.

You're not. After saying hello to our niece, then we can get everything ready at Layla's cottage. We'll take care of her once the day is over. His dragon paused a second and then added, *And think of it this way—with both the bairns delivered, it won't be long before we can have a frenzy of our own.*

Chase glanced over at an exhausted Faye holding her daughter, with Grant at her side. Some would say he was too young, impulsive, or a thousand other excuses. But as Chase watched his brother with his new family, Chase knew he wanted that, too.

Even if it meant him taking more responsibility at home some days while Layla worked, he wouldn't mind.

His dragon bobbed his head. *Then be the doting uncle and start putting things into motion for it to happen.*

I won't rush Layla into it.

Aye, I know. But if she's as anxious to have the frenzy as we are, then find a way to make it happen. Layla isn't the best person at asking for help, after all.

He'd rather not start speaking for Layla, if he could help it.

But as his mother guided him to Faye's bed and he saw his tiny, dark-haired niece up close for the first time, Chase smiled as he traced her soft, pink cheek, forgetting everything but the tiny bundle in Faye's arms. "Hello, wee Isla. I'm your Uncle Chase. Just know now that I'll be your fun uncle, meaning I'll probably be your favorite, too."

Fraser grunted. "That would be my role, lad."

The other male had tried to put dominance into his voice, but it wasn't enough to stop Chase from grinning and replying, "Then I guess we have a new competition, aye?"

Grant sighed and muttered something Chase didn't hear. Ignoring his brother, he took Isla's tiny hand and whispered, "Don't worry about your dad. He pretends to be serious all the time, but he has a fun side, too. I'll teach you how to bring it out, as well as how to annoy him as much as possible. It'll be great fun, you'll see, Isla."

She moved her mouth, and even though it was probably nothing to do with his words, Chase took it as a sign that she was on board for his plans.

When he finally stepped aside to allow another family member some time with the bairn, Chase glanced to the door. He only hoped everything was going well with Yasmin's labor and birth. He couldn't bear to think of Layla losing her sister only after just finding her.

No. He wouldn't think those kinds of thoughts right now and ruin the atmosphere in the room. So he fawned over his niece for a bit longer before leaving to get things set up inside Layla's cottage. He'd have to be prepared for one of two outcomes—one happy and one devasting—but he'd be ready for either one.

Chapter Sixteen

L ayla was no stranger to long work hours. However, she'd nearly lost Faye MacKenzie earlier in the day, and now her sister was in the tenth hour of labor, too.

Dr. Sid had helped with Faye, but the female doctor now had to take care of an emergency with one of the children. Even the junior doctor was busy, trying to help Aimee King at Cat MacAllister's place.

Which meant Layla would have to draw on every bit of strength she had left to treat her sister's delivery as routine.

Logan had volunteered to help with the delivery and had given her little chance to say no.

So he currently finished setting up the new arrival station, where he'd check out the bairn and ensure he or she was braw and healthy.

Yasmin collapsed at the end of a contraction, and Layla checked to see how dilated Yasmin was. Once done, she stood. "Right, this next time, you're going to push."

"I can't," Yasmin whispered. "I'm so tired."

Considering her sister hadn't been in labor for an overly long period of time—sometimes it could take more than a day for the first bairn to come—it wasn't a good sign and meant Yasmin was still weak from living on the run for so long.

Not allowing fear to creep in, Layla moved up to near her sister's head and stated, "You can do this, Yas. Your wee one is anxious to come out and meet you. All you need is to be strong for a little while longer, and then you can let everyone else spoil you and the bairn for weeks, months even."

Yasmin smiled weakly. "By you?"

Layla snorted. "A wee bit. But through a complicated tangle of matings—including my own, once I get to it—the MacKenzies will claim you, too. And seeing as Faye MacKenzie's daughter was born the same day, I'm sure they'll take it as a sign to be extra special to your son or daughter."

Phillip wiped Yasmin's brow and then kissed it. "You can do it, love. You're one of the strongest people I know. Who else could've survived roughing it for five years and never being caught? Only the cleverest, that's who."

Yasmin frowned. "You're making me out to be more than I am, Phillip. You know full well how much I complained."

"Aye, you did. And yet, you carried on." He continued to stroke Yasmin's brow. "I'm the luckiest male alive, and I'll never forget it, Yasmin. So let's start the next chapter of our lives right here, back on Lochguard. We're home."

"Home," Yasmin murmured right before she sucked in a breath and added, "Another one's coming."

Layla moved back between her sister's legs. "Push, Yas, with everything you have."

She watched her sister's face, in case she had to encourage her more. But Yasmin grunted and tried pushing. As the head became visible, her sister cried out. Since everything looked normal, Layla focused on the bairn. At the sight of the tiny head of her niece or nephew, a crack appeared through the wall between doctor and regular female.

She was about to be an aunt. Well, for the second time in a day.

Her dragon lifted her head from where she'd been snoozing. *Get it together. You can be the auntie later.*

Right. Layla coaxed Yasmin through the next contraction. After a fair bit of grunting, screaming, and pushing, Yasmin managed to get her wee lad out. Layla grinned, stood, and held him up. "You have a son."

Yasmin promptly started crying.

Phillip shot her an encouraging look. "She always said it'd be a boy. She's happy, I promise."

More than aware of how emotional a birth could be, Layla nodded and focused on her nephew. Once the umbilical cord was cut, she wrapped him in a blanket and cuddled him in her arms. "Hello, lad. I'm your auntie," she whispered before settling him in Yasmin's arms.

"He's so beautiful," Yasmin murmured before kissing the bairn's forehead.

"Not a he, love. Jacob."

"Jacob," Yasmin echoed before kissing the lad's forehead again.

Layla had always wondered if she was truly mother material or not. Even knowing she'd have a frenzy with Chase that resulted in a pregnancy, she'd had secret doubts.

However, as she watched her sister and her brother-in-law stare down in awe at their child, Layla yearned to have that, too. A family of her own, one that she'd fight to keep from splitting apart or growing distant, like hers had done.

She only needed to get as much sorted as she could before she could begin that journey.

Her dragon huffed. *Finally. Then you won't put off the frenzy forever?*

No. I may not get everything lined up today, but as soon as I can.

Her dragon snorted. *You have to be the only dragon-shifter in history to plan out their frenzy and schedule it.*

I doubt that's true.

Logan arrived to take the bairn so he could check him over, and Layla focused back on her sister to deliver the afterbirth.

As soon as it was done and she'd cleaned up, she sent Logan to fetch Chase. After all, Jacob would be his nephew soon, too.

Layla finally had the chance to stand next to Yasmin's bed and take a good look at wee Jacob. He looked like most bairns—wrinkly—with a few wisps of dark hair on his head.

Yasmin lifted him up. "Hold him, Layla. For a while, I didn't think he'd ever get to know his auntie. But now that he will, he should know you from the very first hour."

As she took him, she smiled. "I delivered him, remember?"

"Aye, but that's a wee bit traumatic and was only your doctor's side. He needs to know just Layla, my lovely older sister."

Maybe it was the emotions of the day, but Layla had to blink back tears at her sister's words.

Layla rearranged the blanket around Jacob, and he moved a second before settling back down. "Hello, wee Jacob. Your mum thinks we need another first meeting, so here I am."

The baby didn't wake up and just laid there.

Her dragon chuckled. *He's tired. One day, I'm sure everyone will wish for him to calm down a little.*

She hummed a tune and just handed back her nephew when Logan returned. However, Chase wasn't right behind him. "Where's Chase?" she asked.

Logan shook his head. "He can't come right now. You're both needed in Finn's office, and he's waiting for you there."

What could Finn want from them?

Maybe if she weren't so tired—it was becoming harder and harder to merely focus her eyes—she'd be more curious. But for the moment, she just wanted to get it over with so she could go home and curl up in bed with her male.

Layla gave one last look at her sister. "Will you be okay for a bit without me?"

Yasmin smiled. "Go, Layla. After delivering two bairns back-to-back, you need a wee bit of rest. Besides, we'll be fine here with all the nurses and the other doctors."

Since both mother and bairn were in good health for the moment, Layla gave one last glance at her nephew and left the room, heading for Finn's cottage.

CHASE STOOD inside Finn's office, hoping he'd made the right choice about all of this.

But after the events of the day and how close Faye had been to dying—reminding him of how short life could be—he didn't want to wait any longer. He needed to claim Layla as his own. Even if it was only in front of Finn and Arabella, without the clan watching on, he was fine with that.

But he couldn't wait another day to make Layla MacFie his mate.

Finn hung up his call with Stonefire's clan leader and turned to study him. After a beat, Finn stood. "Last chance, lad. Are you sure you can handle being mated to a doctor?"

While he usually got along with Finn, Chase didn't hold back a growl. "Why does everyone keep bloody asking me that? Do I need to wear a T-shirt that says,

'Aye, I can be a doctor's mate' so that people will leave me alone?"

Finn shrugged. "It might help." Chase opened his mouth, but Finn raised a hand and added, "Settle down, lad. I judge more on actions than merely age, but you and Layla have been together less than two weeks. And with what's happening with her parents, I don't want her to jump in without thinking and possibly regret it later."

Fucking fantastic. Finn thought Chase would be a mistake.

He was about to say what he thought of that, but Layla's voice filled the air. "I'd like to think I can make decisions for myself. I'm not exactly what you'd call impulsive," she drawled.

Chase turned around. Just the sight of Layla alive and teasing made his heart swell. He raised a hand, palm up. "Come here, love."

She didn't hesitate to place her hand in his and then raised an eyebrow. "What's this all about anyway?"

Finn chuckled, but Chase ignored him. He took Layla's other hand and pulled her close, until her front pressed against his. "Mate me, Layla, right here, right now, in front of Finn. I love you, and I don't want to wait."

"Chase," she breathed.

Moving a hand to her waist and the other to her cheek, he continued, "We can put off the frenzy as long as you like. But become my mate, Layla. Because life is too short to wait."

Layla smiled slowly, and both man and beast took

notice. Even though her actions already told him her answer, she said, "Aye, I'll mate you right now, Chase."

His gaze dropped to her lips. Damn, it was becoming harder and harder not to kiss his female. He murmured, "When it comes time for the frenzy, I'm going to make sure my dragon behaves long enough to let me kiss my fill of your sweet lips, love."

She blushed, and blood rushed south. He was going to spend the rest of his life making her blush as many times as possible.

Finn cleared his throat. "I hate to rush this, but I need to meet with the Iranian dragons tonight for a dinner meeting of sorts. If you're ready, I'll call Ara in to be another witness."

Never severing eye contact with one another, they nodded in unison.

Chase barely noticed Finn getting Arabella. He was too busy tracing Layla's jaw, her cheek, even the bridge of her nose. He could tell she was tired from the smudges under her eyes, but it didn't make her any less beautiful to him.

Finn finally spoke again, meaning he'd returned. "Then let's begin. In lieu of arm cuffs, you'll have to draw each other's names in the old language for now."

Taking his cue, Chase spoke first as the male, per tradition. "Layla MacFie, I've had the chance to watch you from a distance for two years, observing how much you care for others, give your everything to make them healthy, and have also noticed your daily sacrifices to make it all happen. However, in the last two weeks, I've come to know the lass underneath, the one with her own demons and trials, the one with a hidden sense of humor, and also an oddly innocent female who blushes more than anyone I know. I love everything about you and look forward to teasing you more, forcing you to relax, and simply being the person you can depend on above all others. I love you, Layla MacFie. Will you accept my claim?"

"I do," she murmured.

Taking a marker from Finn, he slowly wrote his name in the old dragon language on her upper arm, the one without the tattoo. Even though man and beast liked the sight, both couldn't wait until she wore the silver arm cuff engraved with their name while naked and screaming in their bed.

Once he finished, Layla spoke. "Chase McFarland, I tried everything to avoid you and put you off. But despite it all, you kept trying, to the point I couldn't help but notice you. When I needed help, you didn't blink an eye to offer. And as you took care of me one time after the other, I finally allowed myself to rely on someone besides myself. Not only that, for the first time in a long time, I want to simply fly somewhere pretty with you, to listen to the melody of the wind whispering through the heather and peaks. I want to live life, with you. You bring out the bits and pieces of myself I rarely show others. And for it, I love you, Chase McFarland. Will you accept my claim?"

He nodded, and she took the marker. However, as she began to write the first letter, she paused and closed her eyes. Chase asked, "What's wrong?"

"Nothing."

His instinct warned otherwise. He watched her

closely, for the slightest change as she finished writing her name on his arm. Was she paler than normal, or was it merely his imagination? For the first time, he wished he had a smidgen of medical training so he could be a better judge.

When Layla tried to lay the marker down, she dropped it on the floor. In the next beat, she leaned against his chest.

Something was definitely wrong. He said softly, "Layla, love, tell us what's happening."

"I-I can't focus. Everything's blurry, and…"

Layla passed out in his arms, but he caught her and kept her upright. As his heart pounded double-time, he slowly eased her to the ground, doing his best to keep it together so he could help his mate.

His brand-new mate, and one he fucking wasn't going to let make him a widower so soon.

Even before he'd finished easing Layla down, Finn was already on her other side. Chase had barely caressed Layla's cheek before his clan leader reached for her neck and placed his fingers on it, searching for a pulse.

Chase willed Finn to find it.

After two seconds, Finn swore.

Chase's stomach dropped. No, no, no. Layla couldn't be dead. She couldn't, not when he'd just finally claimed her.

He pushed Finn's hand out of the way to check for himself, but the clan leader gripped his wrist and stated, "She's alive. But her heartbeat is weak. You stay here and talk to her. Convince her to hang on whilst I'll get Dr. Sid."

She was alive. He repeated the statement inside his head as a lifeline. Now all he had to do was ensure she stayed that way.

And even if he had to move mountains to do it, Chase would find a way to save his female.

Finn left, but he barely noticed, leaning down to kiss Layla's jaw, her cheek, her forehead, anywhere he could. His lass had always craved his touch, and so Chase continually stroked her with his hands and caressed her face with his lips to let her know he was there.

His dragon said, *Talk to her, order her, something. She can't leave us. She can't.*

He willed his voice not to crack as he ordered, "Layla, love, stay with us. Sid will help you soon enough. Don't you dare make me a widower this soon, damn it. Stay alive, love. There are so many places I want to show you, so many laughs I want to coax from your bonny mouth. Please, Layla, hang on."

His mate didn't move, twitch, nothing to show she'd heard him.

But he wasn't going to give up. She was the greatest prize of his life, so he tried loving words, arguing one-sided, and ordering her some more. He tried anything and everything to get her attention.

And yet none of it worked.

Tears built up in his eyes as Layla's skin grew a little cooler. Only the sight of her chest rising and falling kept both man and beast from going crazy. As long as she breathed, she could come back to him.

He didn't know how long he sat there, ordering Layla

to stay alive and wake up. Eventually, Dr. Sid rushed in, pushed him aside, and began examining Layla.

A nurse also crouched down and it all became a blur of orders, needles, and various things he didn't know the name of.

But when Dr. Sid started giving heart compressions, Chase's own heart stopped beating.

Layla could die, could leave him, could never have the happy life of love and laughter she'd deserved.

He needed to be at her side again, telling her to stay.

Chase tried to get to his mate, but Finn had returned and held him back. Not caring that Finn was his leader, Chase leaned forward, elbowed the male at his back, and even kicked him. "She needs me. Let me go!"

And yet Finn still held him and murmured, "Give Sid a chance, Chase. If anyone can save her, it will be her."

The fight faded as anger boiled up. Chase shouted, "Don't you fucking die on me, Layla! You hear? Don't you fucking die!"

And as he watched the doctor try to save his mate, tears finally streamed down Chase's cheeks.

Layla was dying—maybe even already dead—and there was nothing he could do about it.

Chapter Seventeen

Two hours later, Chase was back inside a private waiting room, sitting on the sofa, his head in his hands.

While Dr. Sid had gotten Layla's heart beating again, he didn't know anything else beyond it. No one had come to update him. Not even to say if she still lived or died.

The thought of Layla still, her body cooling as life left her, made him want to destroy every piece of furniture in the room. Hell, in the bloody surgery.

Chase had felt helpless before, but nothing compared to his mate hovering on death's door and him sitting in a bloody waiting room, unable to do a fucking thing.

His mother placed a hand on his shoulder. "Dr. Sid is one of the best dragon doctors. She'll help your mate, no question, Chase."

His mum had kept saying such things for the last hour, ever since his brother had brought her to the waiting room. Chase knew it was supposed to give him hope, but it was becoming harder and harder not to snap.

And when he realized that, he felt like an arse. His mum had lost her mate for good. Maybe not through death, but it hadn't been any less painful. He could at least dredge up some patience and be kind. "I hope so, Mum."

His dragon spoke up. *Layla is a fighter and strong. She'll pull through.*

Not you, too.

Would you rather I give up on her? Because I won't.

He mentally sighed. *I know. I'm just afraid of the worst.*

The door opened, and his brother walked in. Chase glanced up at Grant. "Any news?"

"Dr. Sid is on her way here. All I know is that Layla's still alive."

Thank fuck, he murmured to both himself and his dragon.

Of course, alive was only part of the equation. He still didn't know what was wrong with his mate.

He nodded at his brother. "Thanks for the update, Grant. You can go back to Faye and the bairn."

His brother moved to sit next to him, on the arm of the sofa. "Faye said if I didn't stay a wee while with you, she'd have me thrown out of the room. So, here I am." Grant placed a hand on Chase's shoulder. "Right now, you need me more."

Chase and his brother had never been overly affectionate with each other. But in that moment, Grant's firm grip on his shoulder gave him an influx of a wee bit of strength.

Dr. Sid burst into the room. They all stood. Once the doctor shut the door, she gave her report. "Layla is stable for now. While her dragon-shifter hormones were low, it wasn't what caused her crash. We're still running tests, but some of her initial bloodwork came back abnormal."

He clenched his fingers into a fist at the non-answer. "Meaning what?"

Dr. Sid didn't blink at his growly tone. "I don't have all the results yet, but all of her symptoms and initial bloodwork makes me think she has a rare blood condition."

He frowned. "Isn't that something she would've known about?"

"If she were human, most likely. But as dragon-shifters move from decade to decade, their bodies change a fraction, sometimes for the better but usually for the worse, beyond simply getting older. If my theory is correct, it probably began not long after she turned thirty. It's purely will that's kept her on her feet for as long as she has been, especially with the hours she works. Not to mention she hasn't had a yearly exam in nearly a decade. If she had, then she would've known to start treatment years ago."

Damn it, Layla. He was going to have to force her to get them from now on, even if he had to sling her over his shoulder and drag her kicking and screaming.

"When will you know for sure if it's this rare blood condition?" Chase asked.

The female doctor didn't miss a beat. "Within the next few hours. But if it is a blood disease, that creates another problem. The medication to treat it is rare and the plant required to make it is difficult to find. In this part of the world, it grows only in the most remote parts of Scotland and Ireland."

"Show me a picture."

Sid frowned. "There's no way you've seen it."

He growled. "I've spent a lot of time over the last two years flying to remote locations to try and distance myself from Layla and resist the true-mate pull. One of my hobbies is collecting plants from everywhere I go. There's a good chance I've seen it and can find it."

It was almost as if fate had steered him to create a secret garden for his doctor mate to use one day.

Even with a skeptical look on her face, the doctor pulled out her mobile phone, tapped it a few times, and turned the screen toward him.

It was a bush covered in red flowers that were shaped like stars.

And aye, he'd noticed it before, on the Isle of Lewis and Harris. He was fairly sure he had one or two of them in his garden. "I've seen it before. If it's in season, then I can fetch some." If not, then, well, he'd rather not think about it. "Is there anything else I should look out for?"

Grant chimed in. "Chase, you should stay here. If you tell me the location, I'll send one of the Protectors."

"No. This is something I can do, and much quicker on my own than trying to describe the place." A place he wanted to save for Layla, once she was better. Because she *would* get better. "Let me help my mate."

"It may not be what she needs, if the test results come back different than I think they will," Dr. Sid stated softly.

"I know that. But I'd rather have it in case Layla needs it."

Dr. Sid bobbed her head. "Then I'll send a few more pictures to your mobile of other possible plants I'll need, in case you see them, too. The more remedies I have available, the better."

Grant interjected. "And Cooper will go with you. Don't argue, it's nonnegotiable."

Cooper was Grant's second-in-command, and Chase knew the male could keep a secret if he asked. "Fine, he can come. But I'm leaving as soon as possible, so have him meet me at the main landing area." He looked back at the doctor. "Can I at least see Layla once, before I leave?"

Sadness flashed in Dr. Sid's eyes. "No, I'm afraid not. I'm still pinpointing the cause, and we're keeping her in a sterile environment and in quarantine until I sort it all out."

He nearly snarled and demanded to see her, but then his dragon murmured, *Dr. Sid would let us see Layla if she could. You know that.*

Now his beast was the calmer of the two. *Aye, I do. But I don't like it.*

Neither do I. But let's focus our energy on getting to our hidden garden as quickly as possible.

After muttering his farewells, Chase walked out of the surgery and straight to the landing area. As he shucked his clothes, he focused on what he could control —shifting into his dragon form and flying as quickly as possible to the south.

Chapter Eighteen

C at MacAllister stared at the closed door of her guest bedroom and willed for Aimee King to have a peaceful night.

The lass had been doing fine, working on one of her paintings, but then a sound of a dragon flying overhead had sent her into a panic. No amount of coaxing had been able to pull the lass out of her nightmare, and so Cat had resorted to calling the doctor.

The doctor had forced her into a medically induced coma, one that should last for a while yet.

She hated that the dragonwoman had to be drugged, but she knew nothing about medicine and trusted the doctor's judgment.

All she hoped now was that the doctor's statement, about Aimee sleeping for a total of forty-eight hours, held true and not just for the female's sake, either. Cat had asked her brother Connor to come over and listen for anything amiss while she ran an errand. Cat didn't want to leave Aimee, but she had a long-standing appointment to keep. And when the Department of Dragon Affairs reached out to a person about spearheading a project, a dragon-shifter simply didn't say no.

Her beast spoke up. *You could reschedule if you wanted. And don't give me the excuse you can't. In reality, you just want to see* him *again.*

Cat resisted looking to the room she used as her studio, where more than one painting featured the male in question. *If I want to see him again, it's only to refresh my memory and memorize more details of his face and form to improve my next painting.*

Her dragon snorted. *Right, tell yourself that.*

A knock sounded at the front door. Ignoring her beast, she opened it to find her younger, but much taller brother Connor. She motioned him inside.

Since Cat was the eldest of five, she couldn't help but stand up a wee bit straighter and put a touch of dominance in her voice. "Remember what I said, Connor. Don't bother her unless absolutely necessary. I know you think you're a gift to all females, but she's having a difficult time and doesn't do well with males. Leave her be."

Connor raised a dark eyebrow. "I'm not ten years old, Cat. And I'm not a gift to all females." He placed a hand over his heart. "Females who fancy females will always just miss out on all of this."

She rolled her eyes. "You only say that now because Jade and her long-time girlfriend turned you down. As I recall, they laughed at the idea of sharing your bed, to the point they both started crying."

He shrugged, pretending it didn't bother him in the

least. However, Cat had noticed the split-second flattening of his lips before he'd forced a smile again. "It just gives me more energy for those who could appreciate a bloke like me."

Feeling a headache coming on, Cat turned from her brother and picked up her bag. "Aye, aye, you're so brilliant and fit, I know." She glanced over her shoulder. "But I'm your sister and I know full well there's a kind, caring heart inside that chest, underneath all the swagger. If you're not careful, I may even share a secret or two about your time caring for our old Auntie Maude."

Connor growled. "If you tell anyone I put together a fancy high tea for our auntie, I'll just happen to share a photo I snapped of that painting, the one with your half-naked human."

She turned around with a frown. "When were you in my studio? Not only is it off-limits, but I also lock it anytime I'm not in it."

Her brother grinned. "As if that would keep me out."

What she wanted to do was scold Connor and treat him like a child, not caring that he was twenty-three years old. However, she needed to leave in the next minute or two if she didn't want to be late for her meeting. And considering Lachlan MacKintosh was Mr. Punctual to the extreme, she didn't want to give him the satisfaction of her being late.

Not that she always tried to be tardy, but sometimes Cat lost track of time when it came to drawing, painting, or even daydreaming.

She glared a second at Connor and then murmured, "We'll talk about this later. Just be nice and quiet with Aimee here, aye? I should be back in an hour or two."

"Of course I'll watch over her, Cat. I can be cheeky, but I'm not a bastard."

She smiled. "I know." Moving toward the door, she gave her brother one last look before exiting her small cottage.

As she made her way toward the Protector's main security building, where the meeting was to be held, her dragon growled before saying, *I don't like that Connor broke into our studio.*

Neither do I, dragon. But scolding him will only provoke him into sharing the photo. So we'll have to tread lightly.

I don't know why you're so worried. It's just a painting.

Aye, but a painting of a human who never gave his permission for us to paint him. And given both his position and his personality, I don't think he'll like it much if he finds out.

Originally, the project had been to make a silly painting, one that would make Lachlan the Serious smile.

But as she'd worked on the thing, it'd turned into something more. Something she'd love to display and show off since it was probably her best work to date. However, it would also raise suspicions about Cat wanting the human male.

And she most definitely didn't need another challenge in her life at the moment, what with her mother not feeling well for the last few months and Cat having to help out more and more at her mum's restaurant. Lachlan may be sexy in his own quiet, reserved way, but she didn't have time to find out what made the human so reserved and strung tight.

After helping to raise and take care of her four siblings, Cat was tired of trying to heal and look after others. Maybe if she found the right male, that would change. But Lachlan was most definitely not the male for her.

She finally arrived at the security building and made her way to the first conference room, which was always the one used for human visitors, to avoid giving too much of the building's layout away. Stopping at the door, she greeted Iris, one of the higher-up Protectors. "Hello, Iris. Is he here yet?"

"Aye, although I wouldn't be surprised if he hasn't worn a hole in the floor from all his pacing."

She murmured her thanks, took a deep breath, and walked in.

Lachlan MacKintosh stopped on the far side of the room in mid-pace, and she had to blink. He'd changed in the nearly nine months since she'd last seen him.

Aye, he'd been strong enough before, but he now had muscled biceps to rival that of a dragon-shifter. Not only that, his hair was softer, a touch lighter from either time somewhere sunny or he'd highlighted his hair.

Her dragon snorted. *I doubt he'd sit still in a salon.*

Given his tanned skin, Cat agreed it was probably from the sun. And most definitely not from being in the UK either since it was winter.

He raised an eyebrow in question but said nothing. The action snapped her back to the purpose of the meeting. "If you're waiting for an apology about me being two minutes late, you're not going to get one."

"I wasn't expecting an apology. But you were staring, and I was curious as to why."

The male and his infernal politeness. "You're fishing for a compliment, aren't you?"

He shrugged his well-defined shoulders. "No. But aye, I'm different from before. Considering how much I'm going to be working with dragon-shifters in the coming months, I decided to better prepare myself, in case the worst happens."

Once she shut the door, she asked slowly, "What sort of assignment requires you to train up like that?"

"My answer will depend on how this meeting goes."

She resisted narrowing her eyes at his vague statement. If she could handle her younger siblings—Connor and Jamie in particular—then she could certainly handle one polite, arrogant human male.

Cat pulled out a chair, sat down, and crossed one leg over another, readjusting her long skirt as she did so. "Well? I'm here, so aren't you going to start? As I recall, you love keeping everything to a timetable."

She swore his lips twitched, but if so, it was gone before she could blink, replaced by his usual firmly closed lips.

Lips she'd painted several times, never seeming to get right the fullness of the bottom and slightly less so of the top.

Not wanting to think of what those lips could do if they were on a more agreeable male, she tilted her head in question.

Lachlan didn't sit, but finally replied, "The smaller

exhibition you participated in last year was mostly a success."

Mostly was right. There had been a bomb threat at one point, and they'd had to shut it down early.

He continued, "The DDA Director wants to have a more involved project, one involving both humans and dragon-shifter artists, forming a collective of sorts."

Her heart skipped a beat. She'd dreamed of one day working side by side with other artists but always had to put the idea on hold to help out her mother and siblings.

Of course, the reasons she still had to help her family hadn't changed. Her elation faded a fraction, since it'd probably be held far away for her to attend. "Where would this collective meet?"

"The original location was a toss-up between London and Glasgow."

As she'd suspected, both places were too far away to fly to, attend a meeting, and return in a day.

She opened her mouth to say she couldn't go to those places, but Lachlan didn't give her the chance. "However, your clan leader apprised me of your responsibilities here, and how those places wouldn't be possible if you're to participate. After negotiating with Mr. Stewart, he and I have come to a deal. The collective will meet here, on Lochguard, with occasionally longer stays allowed for the visiting artists."

She blinked. "On Lochguard?"

"Aye."

She eyed his muscled arms. "I'm not sure you needed to train up to stay on with my clan. We're tied with

Stonefire for friendliest dragon clan to humans in the UK."

"Since I'll be living here for a short while, conducting tours, exhibitions, and lectures with both humans and dragon-shifters, I wanted to be prepared."

"Wait, what? You're going to live here?"

Her dragon hummed. *Good. Then you can study him as much as you want. And maybe even try him out once or twice, to give me some sex. It'll also help make your paintings more realistic, so it's a win-win.*

Lachlan replied before she could scold her beast. "Aye, that's what I said. Come summer, I'll arrive to get everything set up and ready. The other artists will begin arriving in the autumn." Lachlan took a step forward. "You are to be my main coordinator on Lochguard. And before you say you can't do it, your clan leader is establishing a schedule for others to help out at your family's restaurant."

"In other words, I can't say no."

He raised his brows. "Why would you want to?"

She mirrored his facial expression. "Do you like for others to make decisions for you?"

He took two steps closer, and Cat did her best not to watch how his arms swung, or how his trousers pulled against his muscled thighs.

Placing his hands on the table, he leaned on them and asked, "Sometimes, aye, I do. Especially when it's clearly something that could help so many people."

And there he went making her feel selfish and about ten years old.

Because working with human artists, allowing tours,

and maybe even one day bringing children together to create a mural or some such thing, would do a world of good. Treaties, contracts, and laws were one way to enact long-lasting social change. However, art and culture was another.

Her dragon grunted. *Would you really say no, just because he made the decision for you?*

Of course not.

Then just tell him we'll do it.

In just a second.

Cat stood, and Lachlan did the same. "If I agree to this, you promise me this is the last time you make a decision for me. We work together, you ask, and then we move forward. Maybe some people are afraid of your higher-up position with the DDA, but not me." She allowed her eyes to flash to slits and back on purpose, but to his credit, the human didn't so much as blink. "Do we have an understanding?"

Maybe some would gasp at the way she handled the human, but she'd learned from a young age with her siblings that if she didn't set boundaries early, they almost never held later.

And while she loved her siblings regardless of how out of hand they could be, this human male was unrelated. Not to mention in the grander scheme of things, she suspected he needed her more than the other way around.

Never breaking her gaze, Lachlan moved around the table to stand next to her. She hated that she had to look up to see his face. After all, he was only a *human*. And humans weren't supposed to be taller than her.

Okay, maybe some of them were. But she didn't want him to be because that only tempted her more.

And she couldn't be tempted. Her family, and now Aimee King, depended too much on her.

As they stared at one another, Cat's heart rate jumped. She'd never had someone focus solely on her with such intensity before.

When Lachlan finally spoke, his voice was rough. "Together, then. But remember, dragonwoman, that ultimately I am the one in charge."

She sensed a double meaning in his words, but before she could say more, he added, "I'll send over the paperwork to you later today. Reach out to my assistant if you have any questions."

With that, he exited the room in a few long strides.

Cat let out a long breath. What the bloody hell had that been all about?

And why did she want him to come back so she could match wits and find out?

Pushing the thought aside, she exited the room and headed back to her cottage. She'd deal with Lachlan MacKintosh when the time came. For now, others needed her, and Cat wasn't going to let them down.

Chapter Nineteen

L ayla vaguely heard some females' voices as she
slowly woke up.

"Come on now, Faye. Wouldn't it be fantastic? To
think, your daughter could mate the male born the same
day as her. That'll be quite the story to tell later on."

"Mum, I'm *not* going to plan out Isla's future for her.
So just stop it." A pause. "Right, Yasmin?"

"Aye."

It was Faye, Yasmin, and Lorna MacKenzie.

But was Chase there?

Her dragon was weak inside her head. *We need to open
our eyes and look around. We can do it.*

It should be an easy thing to do, open her eyes. And
yet it took several minutes of concentration to get them
cracked even a fraction.

Maybe she could've done it sooner, but Faye and her
mother continued to bicker, and Layla did her best to
block it out. Concentrating in general was difficult, and

she didn't want to waste energy on a pointless conversation.

She finally managed to get them open and it took a few seconds to focus. All Layla could tell was that she was in a bed inside one of the rooms of her surgery.

As she tried to make her mouth work, Yasmin gasped and her face came into view. "Layla! You're awake!"

She couldn't manage more than a groan.

Faye's head came into view. "She is. Mum, go get Chase."

Chase. Aye, she wanted to see him. Maybe he'd tell her the truth of what had happened. The others might eventually, but Layla most likely wouldn't stay awake long, and she'd probably have to ask a lot of questions to get the females to share everything.

Faye spoke again. "Can you talk, Layla?"

She finally croaked, "A little."

Faye grinned. "You'll be fine, just like I thought. And I think the bairn healing vibes helped, too."

If she had more energy, Layla would frown.

Thankfully, Yasmin spoke up before Faye spouted more nonsense. "Save your strength, Layla. Chase will be here soon. And aye, I know you love us, too. But he needs to see you more, I think. He's as devoted to you as Phillip is to me."

She debated whether it was worth it to ask for more information on Yasmin's cryptic statement when Chase rushed into the room and came into view. Even with a few days' worth of stubble and bloodshot eyes, he was as sexy as ever.

He gently stroked her face, each stroke relaxing her a fraction. "Layla, love, you've come back."

He gently kissed her forehead, the action making her fight to ask, "What happened?"

Chase caressed her cheek as he answered, "You nearly died, love. But you're better and should be fine. Dr. Sid said if you woke up, then the danger had passed."

She frowned. Died? One minute she'd been finishing her mate vows with Chase, and the next she'd woken up here.

As if reading her mind, he continued, "You have a rare blood condition, love. One that can be managed, but you'd been living with it for years without any medication." He frowned. "You're not going another six months without a physical exam ever again."

Faye chimed in. "Not like she's going to be able to avoid seeing a doctor for more than a few weeks at a time for the foreseeable future, anyway."

Chase growled at his sister-in-law. "Faye, that wasn't your secret to share."

"Secret?" Layla croaked.

Chase glanced at her a second before glaring at the other two females. "Right now, I want to have a private conversation with my mate."

Faye sighed. "Fine, fine. We'll be off. The bairns did their magic already, anyway."

"I'll come back later, Layla," Yasmin added.

Once they both collected their sleeping children from the tiny crib off to the side of the room, Faye and Yasmin shuffled off. Layla whispered, "What is she talking about? Magic?"

Chase shook his head. "Faye believed bringing your niece and nephew into the room would help bring you back. Something about their cuteness being too hard to ignore, meaning you'd have to wake up to notice it at some point."

She smiled weakly.

Chase caressed her face, each strum of his fingers making her feel a wee bit more alive.

He finally leaned down and kissed her lips.

She widened her eyes, waiting for the mate-claim frenzy to course through her.

And it didn't.

He finally pulled away. "Layla, love, you carry our bairn, which is why there's no frenzy—we'll have to make one ourselves someday." Chase paused to kiss her once more before adding softly, "Dr. Sid's still unsure if you'll be able to carry to term, but I know how stubborn my lass can be. And I know everything will be all right in the end."

A million thoughts whirled through her head. Pregnant? With a rare blood condition? Depending on which one, she might never be able to ever have a child. Would that devastate Chase?

"Layla."

Chase garnered her attention again. He continued, "We'll figure this all out together, love. You have all the doctors of the UK ready to help if needed—a few in Ireland from Clan Glenlough, too—Dr. Sid ensured that. Add in me, even though I'm rubbish at anything related to medicine, and all of us will support you, no matter what happens."

Tears threatened to fall. After so many years of not having help, she was going to have more than she ever imagined.

And none of it would've ever happened if not for a young, sexy dragonman bringing her coffee at the surgery, coming back no matter how much she tried to ignore him.

She blurted, "I love you, Chase."

"I love you, too, Layla MacFie."

"McFarland," she stated. "I'm Layla McFarland now. I want your name, not my father's."

Chase cupped her cheek and kissed her gently. "Then you have it, Dr. McFarland. With you as head doctor and Grant as one of the head Protectors, we just need one of us lot as clan leader, and we'll rule it all."

She rolled her eyes, and he laughed.

"Okay, lass, we'll leave that to our bairn someday, aye? Because we know I'm not cut out for it."

Pushing aside the doubt they may not ever have one, she replied, "No, you're not."

"You just want me all to yourself, aye?" He leaned closer. "And I'm okay with that, as I'm a bit selfish myself and want more time to spend with you."

Even though part of Layla yearned to know every last detail of what had happened since she fell unconscious, in that moment, she merely ordered, "Kiss me again, Chase."

He lowered his head and took her lips once more, this time coaxing them apart. As his tongue stroked slowly against hers, she moaned at the delicious taste of her male after so long without.

And he continued to kiss her until she felt sleepy. Even then, Chase sat next to her bed and held her hand as she drifted asleep next to the male who had shifted her entire world for the better.

SOMETIME THE NEXT DAY, Layla found herself sitting upright, eating her meal with gusto when Sid waltzed into the room.

And aye, she waltzed. Sid never seemed to merely walk. That was a trick Layla would need to figure out herself someday.

The dragonwoman sat beside her bed, took off the stethoscope around her neck, and laid it in her lap. She asked without preamble, "Feeling better?"

"Aye, I can probably get out of bed tomorrow."

"That's up to me, of course. But as long as you take your medication every day, you should lead a normal life, for the most part."

For the most part, being the key phrase. Layla's condition made it hard to carry a bairn to term. And it was dangerous to have more than one.

Chase had repeated ad nauseam that she was strong, and one was enough. He'd gladly leave the repopulating of the clan to the MacKenzies.

And if they had none, he didn't care, either. She was all he wanted.

Her dragon growled. *Don't dare cry again.*

I can't help it. Why that male chose me, I'll never fully understand it.

Because we're brilliant?

Sid's voice prevented Layla from replying. "But I'm not here to give orders or the like. I think it's time we finally have that chat since I suspect Chase will be keeping you all to himself once you're out of here."

For once, Layla managed not to blush at the memories of what Chase had promised her once she was cleared for sex again. Instead, she focused on the older dragonwoman. "If you're going to tell me I need to rely on others, slow down, and not work myself to death, I think almost dying has more than convinced me of that."

Sid tilted her head. "I suspected that already. What I don't understand is why you never reached out to Gregor. I understand not knowing me as well and hesitating a little, but he was your mentor, your teacher, and he cares for you like a little sister. Why didn't you ask him for help?"

She bit her lip but pushed past her years-long hesitation to admit weaknesses and faults. "Because it's harder for a female doctor. I'm sure you understand that. But I didn't want to be seen as weaker, lesser, name your adjective here. I wanted to prove I was as good as him. There's been a lot of change on Lochguard in the last few years, and the clan needed strength and dependability."

"Maybe. And yes, it's harder for females to do anything in dragon-shifter culture, if they don't want to merely mate and have babies. I've experienced it myself. However, if you work yourself to death, what does it accomplish? I probably came even closer to killing myself than you did, honestly. If not for Gregor, I probably would be dead by now. And not just because of my

formerly silent dragon and the madness attached to it."
Sid leaned forward and searched Layla's gaze. "Just know
that if you try to pull the shit you've been doing again, I'll
come up here and prescribe bed rest. I may have to
anyway, with the baby, but even if he or she is ten years
old, I'll do it in a heartbeat. And if you think I'm bluffing,
try it." She smiled. "Gregor can tell you how that works
out."

Even with the threats, Layla liked Sid Jackson. "I'll be
good, I promise. I'm sure Chase will set me straight
before you do anyway."

Sid leaned back again and snorted. "If Finn doesn't
do it first. I suspect everyone will be watching you closely,
going forward. Not because you're weak, but because a
lot of people care about you, Layla."

A knock on the door sounded, and Sid shouted,
"Come in."

Layla blinked as Gregor walked into the room, a wee
bundle in his arms. "Gregor," she murmured.

"Aye, it's me, Layla. I've also brought my wee son,
Wyatt, to meet you. He's met just about everyone else,
except you. And if you hadn't taken over Lochguard for
me, I may never have had him or Cassidy to call my own.
So he most definitely needs to meet you, lass."

She smiled. Gregor was the only one to dare call Dr.
Sid by her full first name. "It was nothing."

"It was bloody more than nothing." Sid cleared her
throat, and his frown vanished. "But I didn't come to
argue."

Gregor placed sleeping Wyatt in her arms. She

smiled at the lad before meeting Gregor's gaze again. "He's so well-behaved. He must get that from Sid."

Gregor grunted, but Sid snorted and said, "I think you and I need to become better friends, Layla."

Gregor growled, "I'm not sure I like that idea."

As the three of them laughed and talked a wee while about everything and nothing, Layla realized how much she missed not only her old boss and his humor, but it was also nice to have several someones to discuss medicine and her work with.

Her dragon huffed. *Then make sure to call them more often.*

Aye, I will, dragon. Once I'm out of this bed, I have a whole slew of changes to make.

Some would take time, maybe years, but she was done pretending she didn't need help, let alone hiding everything about herself except for the doctor side. Layla wanted more time with her mate, her sister, and even talking with Sid and Gregor.

And in order to do that, it meant relying on more people and setting up the surgery to run smoothly, even if she wasn't there every single day.

Chapter Twenty

C hase drove the final mile down the dirt road before parking the car he'd borrowed from the Protectors. He glanced at Layla. "We're here."

She wasted no time in getting out of the car, and Chase did the same.

After three long weeks, Dr. Sid had finally cleared Layla to go on the outing. However, until the bairn was born, Layla wasn't allowed to fly. It was too risky. Hence, him having to make the drive.

His dragon huffed. *All I want to do is fly with our mate. First, we waited to have her, and now this.*

Aye, and much like waiting to have her, it'll be worth the wait. There's no way I'll put the bairn's life at risk, let alone Layla's.

And since they both wanted to try their hardest to keep their child, Layla had agreed to the conditions, even if she didn't particularly like them.

Once Chase reached Layla, he put an arm around her waist and drew her against his side. "Are you sure you don't want to wear a blindfold and make the reveal overly dramatic?"

She glanced up at him. "So I can trip, crash into some tree, and then have to rush back to Lochguard?"

He kissed her nose. "I know, I know, we want to avoid any extra work for you."

Leaning her head on his shoulder, she replied, "It's more than that, though. I just want to enjoy the day off with my male. And I'd be lying if I didn't say I'm dying to see this garden of yours. It saved my life, after all."

The basis of her medication was made from a flower he grew. "And I hope to expand it, so it can save other lives. I may not be able to perform a surgery or diagnose a disease, but I know how to grow plants. After today, you can tell me what else it needs, and I'll do my best to provide it."

She squeezed his side. "Then let's hurry up. The sooner we arrive, the sooner you can take your shirt off and start digging, or weeding, or some other sort of manual labor that'll allow me to ogle your sweaty chest and back."

He snorted as he guided her down the somewhat hidden pathway to his garden. "It's bloody cold outside, Layla. As much as I wouldn't mind my female taking care of me when I'm sick, I'd prefer to wait a wee while." He lowered his mouth to her ear. "After all, today is the first time I can have you in weeks."

She glanced up at him, heat in her eyes. "Maybe you should've taken care of that before dragging me into the middle of nowhere, in the dead of winter."

He grinned. "I said I have a few surprises, didn't I?

Now, come on, so I can start revealing them to my curious lass."

As they continued to walk slowly—he wasn't going to push Layla too hard, even if she had been deemed healthy again—he stroked Layla's side, reveling in her heat and scent at his side. Merely having her to himself, without doctors and nurses—let alone family—looking on was pure bliss. Aye, they had a lifetime ahead of them, but Chase would never get enough of his female.

It didn't take more than a few beats before Layla asked, "How did you find this place?"

"As I mentioned before, I needed something to distract me from a beautiful lass destined to be mine, but who didn't give me a second glance. And as I grew tired of flying here and there, with no destination in mind, I asked Finn if I could use one of the abandoned game hunting forests for a special project. Since I had quite the reputation for trouble back then, I had to tell him it was for nothing more troublesome than a garden. He granted the request and promised to keep it secret. And every week, I tried to do a bit more, always adding or clearing a new section. However, it's no longer an escape merely for me. I want it to be our secret place, away from everything else, where we're nothing but two mates in love."

And maybe one day, he could teach his son or daughter to help him. If he and Layla were lucky enough to have one.

If not, he'd be fine with Layla reading a book as he worked, content that his mate was nearby.

Layla sighed. "That sounds lovely." She glanced up. "Although I hope you don't expect me to start stripping my shirt off and digging with a shovel, too. It's not vain to say these hands are worth too much to risk damaging or maiming by mistake."

He smiled down at her. "Of course not, love. Your admiring gaze is all I need."

She beamed up at him, and even though he burned to show her the place, he stopped a second to take her lips in a slow, lingering kiss.

Even though he'd done it thousands of times by now, he never got enough of Layla's sweet taste.

When he finally pulled back, both man and beast stood a little taller at her swollen lips and flushed cheeks.

Layla murmured, "That kiss almost makes me wish we could stop right here and celebrate your secret garden with some mind-blowing sex."

He ran a hand down to her arse and squeezed. "Don't tempt me, love. Don't tempt me." It took herculean effort, but he turned her back toward the path. "Come on. We're nearly there."

EVEN THOUGH LAYLA burned to see Chase's garden, it was hard to be next to her sexy male, feeling his warmth and inhaling his scent, and not think about what they could be doing inside their cottage instead.

Today was the first day she'd been cleared to have sex again, and even if there wasn't a mate-claim frenzy, she wanted to let go and claim her male like there was no tomorrow.

Her dragon snorted. *And they say males are bad.*

Oh, stop it. You're as eager as I am to claim him.

I wouldn't mind sucking his cock before riding it, but I'm not about to do it outside in the bloody cold.

I thought dragons weren't supposed to be as affected by the cold?

Aye, if we're in dragon form. But we take our male when human, and it's freezing. Besides, males shrink up in the cold, and I want all of him inside us, every last inch.

Thinking of how she could reply to that, Chase stopped and murmured, "I'm going to put my hand over your eyes for a few feet. Don't worry, I won't let you fall, lass."

Trusting Chase with her life, she closed her eyes. It was awkward trying to walk on a dirt path without seeing it, but after a few minutes, he murmured, "Wait right here and keep your eyes closed."

She bobbed her head before she heard Chase race away. She shuffled her feet, trying her best to stay warm. Finally, he shouted, "Open them!"

Layla complied and gasped.

White fairy lights were strung around the trees and along the fences on each side, the lights ending toward the back, where they framed the overhang of a small cabin.

It was almost as if the garden and cabin were bathed in starlight.

Chase raced over and smiled down at her. "So you like it?"

She couldn't tear her gaze away, finding new lights in some of the bushes and even around a chair outside the cabin. "It's beautiful. But where did the cabin come from? I know you can be handy, but I don't think you could've built it within a few short weeks."

He grinned. "Aye, you're right, as much as I wish I could build something that fast. The cabin was here already, but just needed some updating, mainly electrical and the roof." He pulled her close against his front. "I wanted a place for you to be able to escape and simply enjoy yourself. This is our little place away from everyone, love. And Finn said we could have it for as long as we like."

Raising a hand, she cupped his cheek. "You're spoiling me again."

"Aye, and I'll continue to do so, so get used to it."

Leaning more against him, she looped both her hands behind his neck. "I suppose that means I should reward you, aye?"

His pupils flashed. "A nobler male would say he didn't need a reward. But there's a bed inside the cabin with our names on it, and I think it deserves some use."

As his lips descended on hers, Layla moaned and instantly let his tongue inside her mouth. As he stroked, she matched him, digging her nails into his neck.

When he moved a hand to her arse and rocked her against his erection, she managed to pull away and say, "As lovely as your garden is, I second the bed."

"Good." He scooped her up and carried her toward the cabin.

She kissed his neck, his chin, his jaw, the air turning too hot despite the frigid temperatures.

Somehow Chase opened the door and carried her inside. The next moment she was on the bed, her male above her, his eyes flashing wildly. "I think it's time to create our own frenzy, Dr. McFarland."

Layla laid her hands above her head and arched her back. "I think so, too, Mr. McFarland."

With a growl, Chase tore off her clothing and then his own before playing out the fantasy he'd voice many times over the last few weeks.

It was even better in real life, but she suspected anything would be better with Chase, the male she loved more than anything else in the world.

Epilogue

Many Months Later

Layla gazed down at the two wee bundles in her arms and couldn't stop crying.

Aye, they were early and small, but they were healthy.

And she was finally a mum.

She choked on a sob, and Chase laid his cheek against hers, murmuring, "Love, it's okay. You'll handle twins just fine. You have me to help you, remember."

"No." *Sniffle.* "It's not that."

Chase wrapped his arms under hers, helping to hold their sons. "Then what's wrong, love? Tell me. I can't stand you crying."

She leaned into Chase's face. "I-I didn't know if we'd ever get here."

Layla had had a difficult pregnancy, to the point she'd been on bed rest for the last three months.

They'd both learned early that she was having twins. Sid had told her she needed to know as soon as possible, in order to be more careful and keep them to term.

She'd nearly lost them once, but between Chase's dedication, as well as the help of more doctors than any one person would need, she'd made it through.

And now she held two tiny, beautiful sons in her arms.

Chase nuzzled her cheek. "But they're both here, you're healthy, and I'm sure one day you'll wonder why you ever wanted children in the first place."

"Never," she answered with a sniffle. "Both of them will always know they're loved and wanted."

"Of course they are. Although I suspect their cousins will occasionally try to lose them in the woods, or who knows what. The MacKenzies are good at stirring up trouble, after all."

The MacKenzies were up to six offspring, plus Finn and Arabella's three. Not to mention Yasmin's son, and her sister was already pregnant with another.

Aye, her sons would have more cousins than they knew what to do with. And Layla couldn't think of a more perfect future, full of love, teasing, and lots of laughter.

She glanced from one bairn to the other, always noticing a new detail when she did. "At least they're not identical, so that should make things a wee bit easier."

One had her dark hair, and the other had the palest wisps on his head, taking after his father's blond.

Chase kissed her cheek before asking, "So which will be which, then?"

"Since we each picked a name, how about we name the one with the same hair color as ours?"

He snorted. "Such an arbitrary way to do it."

"Do you have a better way?"

"No." He touched the dark-haired lad. "Hello, Caelan." And then the blond-haired one. "And Harris. We've waited a long time to meet you."

As Caelan made some motions with his mouth, Layla nodded toward Harris. "Take him for a wee while, Chase. I need to try feeding Caelan."

Commotion sounded outside the door, and Chase sighed as he picked up one of their sons. "We can't keep them out much longer, love. Dr. Sid gave us some time alone, but they'll break the door down before soon, not caring whose wrath they'll face."

As Layla exposed her breast and tried to get her son to suckle, she replied, "Then let them in."

Chase growled, "I don't want them seeing any part of you naked."

Caelan nearly latched but failed. Layla tried again. "They're all mated and devoted to their females. Just tell them to be quiet."

He raised his brows at her. "You're aware that most of them are MacKenzies, aye? Asking them to be quiet is like asking a dragon to cut off their wings."

"Chase," she scolded.

"Aye, aye, I get it. Although it's not going to be a long visit. You may be a doctor, but right now, I'm in charge of your health."

She couldn't help but smile as Chase went to the door. Maybe some females didn't like an overprotective male, but Layla secretly loved it after so many years of doing everything on her own.

Gently caressing her son's cheek, she tried again and finally got Caelan to latch. The feeling was still a bit strange, but for that second, it was only her and her son, the rest of the world vanished. "My wee Caelan. Your mum will always be here to watch over you, no matter what."

Then the door opened and the peaceful quiet disappeared.

Yasmin and Faye were at her side first. Faye did try to keep her voice quiet, which Layla knew couldn't be easy for the female. "Look at how wee he is. I remember when Isla was that small. Now she's walking before learning to crawl, and I can barely keep up with her."

Yasmin smiled. "He's bonnie, Layla. What's his name?"

"This is Caelan. And Chase has Harris."

"Caelan and Harris McFarland," Yasmin echoed. "Lovely, uncommon names."

Layla chuckled. "Aye, well, we don't need another Jamie in the clan, that's for sure. Besides, there's something about calling your child's name and not having four heads turn around when you do."

Grant, the MacKenzie twin males, their mates, and Aunt Lorna—she'd insisted Layla call her that—and her mate, Ross, all crowded around the bed. Finn and Arabella hung back toward the door, fawning over the bundle in Chase's arms.

As Layla made the introductions again, she finally caught Chase's eyes across the room. Love and happiness filled them, and he mouthed, "I love you."

She did the same, right before Caelan let go and cried.

As she tended to her son—it was still surreal to think she was a mum now—Layla was the happiest she'd ever been in her life. After two decades of living as a ghost of herself, she was surrounded by family and love. And while she didn't know exactly what the future held, as long as she had Chase, her sons, and even her newfound family, it would be perfect.

Author's Note

I hope you enjoyed Layla and Chase's story! Originally I planned their story to be a novella. But somehow it morphed into a full-length book, with more than a few surprises that not even I knew were coming. (My characters only reveal things to me when they feel like it!) There's not a lot of action, per se, in *The Dragon's Pursuit*, but it expands the dragon universe even more with the Iranian clans. By now I'm sure you're starting to understand the big picture of where I'm going. :)

You get an even bigger glimpse of this with the three-book dragon spinoff series coming this year, the one set in the USA. There were simply too many US dragon-shifters and clans to write one book in my Stonefire Dragons Universe series, and so the Tahoe Dragon Mates series was born. True, the US stories are shorter and steamy, but it makes for a fun break from everything else going on. I hope you give Jose and Tori a chance in *The Dragon's Choice*.

As for what's next on Lochguard, you'll finally get to see Cat MacAllister and Lachlan MacKinnon get together. I hinted at them back in *The Dragon Warrior*. But never fear, I didn't forget about them! My goal is to have *The Dragon Collective* out in 2021, but I always try to keep the most up-to-date information on my website.

And now, I have some people to thank for getting this out into the world:

- To Becky Johnson and her team at Hot Tree Editing. They always keep a sharp eye and don't hesitate to ask if ripping panties are really that easy.
- To Clarissa Yeo of Yocla Designs. She is amazing at cover design and this one is no exception.
- To all my beta readers—Sabrina D., Donna H., Sandy H., and Iliana G., you do an amazing job at finding those lingering typos and minor inconsistencies.

And as always, a huge thank you to you, the reader, for sticking with me. Writing is the best job in the world and it's your support that makes it so I can keep doing it. If you've read the books and want to support me in another way, almost all of my dragon-shifter audiobooks either are, or will be soon, available in libraries around the globe. Take a listen and enjoy some lovely accents!

Until next time, happy reading! Turn the page for some excerpts of my other works.

PS—To keep up-to-date with new releases and other goodies, please join my newsletter here on www.Jessie-Donovan.com

The Conquest

KELDERAN RUNIC WARRIORS #1

Leader of a human colony planet, Taryn Demara has much more on her plate than maintaining peace or ensuring her people have enough to eat. Due to a virus that affects male embryos in the womb, there is a shortage of men. For decades, her people have enticed ships to their planet and tricked the men into staying. However, a ship hasn't been spotted in eight years. So when the blip finally shows on the radar, Taryn is determined to conquer the newcomers at any cost to ensure her people's survival.

Prince Kason tro de Vallen needs to find a suitable planet for his people to colonize. The Kelderans are running out of options despite the fact one is staring them in the face —Planet Jasvar. Because a group of Kelderan scientists disappeared there a decade ago never to return, his people dismiss the planet as cursed. But Kason doesn't believe in curses and takes on the mission to explore the planet to prove it. As his ship approaches Jasvar, a distress signal chimes in and Kason takes a group down to the planet's surface to explore. What he didn't expect was for a band of females to try and capture him.

As Taryn and Kason measure up and try to outsmart each other, they soon realize they've found their match. The only question is whether they ignore the spark between them and focus on their respective people's survival or can they find a path where they both succeed?

The Conquest Excerpt

CHAPTER ONE

Taryn Demara stared at the faint blip on the decades-old radar. Each pulse of light made her heart race faster. *This is it.* Her people might have a chance to survive.

Using every bit of restraint she had, Taryn prevented her voice from sounding too eager as she asked, "Are you sure it's a spaceship?"

Evaine Benoit, her head of technology, nodded. "Our equipment is outdated, but by the size and movement, it has to be a ship."

Taryn's heart beat double-time as she met her friend's nearly black-eyed gaze. "How long do we have before they reach us?"

"If they maintain their current trajectory, I predict eighteen hours, give or take. It's more than enough time to get the planet ready."

"Right," Taryn said as she stood tall again. "Keep me updated on any changes. If the ship changes course, boost the distress signal."

Evaine raised her brows. "Are you sure? The device is on its last legs. Any boost in power could cause a malfunction. I'm not sure my team or I can fix it again if that happens."

She gripped her friend's shoulder. "After eight years of waiting, I'm willing to risk it. I need that ship to reach Jasvar and send a team down to our planet."

Otherwise, we're doomed was left unsaid.

Without another word, Taryn raced out of the aging technology command center and went in search of her best strategist. There was much to do and little time to do it.

Nodding at some of the other members of her settlement as she raced down the corridors carved into the mountainside, Taryn wondered what alien race was inside the ship on the radar. Over the past few hundred years, the various humanoid additions to the once human-only colony had added extra skin tones, from purple to blue to even a shimmery gold. Some races even had slight telepathic abilities that had been passed down to their offspring.

To be honest, Taryn didn't care what they looked like or what powers they possessed. As long as they were genetically compatible with her people, it meant Taryn and several other women might finally have a chance at a family. The "Jasvar Doom Virus" as they called it, killed off most male embryos in the womb, to the point only one male was born to every five females. Careful genealogical charts had been maintained to keep the gene pool healthy. However, few women were willing to share their partner with others, which meant the male population grew smaller by the year.

It didn't help that Jasvar had been set up as a low-technology colony, which meant they didn't have the tools necessary to perform the procedures in the old tales of women being impregnated without sex. The technique had been called in-something or other. Taryn couldn't remember the exact name from her great-grandmother's stories from her childhood.

Not that it was an option anyway. Jasvar's technology was a hodgepodge of original technology from the starter colonists and a few gadgets from their conquests and alien additions over the years. It was a miracle any of it still functioned.

The only way to prevent the extinction of her people was to capture and introduce alien males into their society. Whoever had come up with the idea of luring aliens to the planet's surface and developing the tools necessary to get them to stay had been brilliant. Too bad his or her name had been lost to history.

Regardless of who had come up with the idea, Taryn was damned if she would be the leader to fail the Jasvarian colony. Since the old technology used to put out the distress signals was failing, Taryn had a different sort of plan for the latest alien visitors.

She also wanted their large spaceship and all of its technology.

Of course, her grand plans would be all for nothing if she couldn't entice and trap the latest aliens first. To do that, she needed to confer with Nova Drakven, her head strategist.

Rounding the last corner, Taryn waltzed into Nova's office. The woman's pale blue face met hers. Raising her silver brows, she asked, "Is it true about the ship?"

With a nod, Taryn moved to stand in front of Nova's desk. "Yes. It should be here in about eighteen hours."

Nova reached for a file on her desk. "Good. Then I'll present the plan to the players, and we can wait on standby until we know for sure where the visiting shuttle lands."

Taryn shook her head and started pacing. "I need you to come up with a new plan, Nova."

"Why? I've tweaked what went wrong last time. We shouldn't have any problems."

"It's not that." Taryn stopped pacing and met her friend's gaze. "This time, we need to do more than entice a few males to stay. Our planet was originally slated to be a low-tech colony, but with the problems that arose, that's no longer an option. We need supplies and knowledge, which means negotiating with the mother ship for their people."

"Let me get this straight—you want to convince the vastly technologically advanced aliens that we are superior, their crew's lives are in danger, and that they need to pay a ransom to get them back?"

Taryn grinned. "See, you do understand me."

Nova sighed. "You have always been crazy and a little reckless."

"Not reckless, Nova. Just forward-thinking. You stage the play, think of a few ideas about how to get the ship, and I'll find a way to make it work."

"Always the super leader to the rescue. Although one day, your luck may run out, Taryn."

Nova and Taryn were nearly the same age, both in their early thirties, and had grown up together. Nova was her best friend and one of the few people Taryn was unafraid to speak her fears with. "As long as my luck lasts through this ordeal, I'm okay with that. I can't just sit and watch our people despairing if another year or ten pass before there's new blood. If we had a way to get a message to Earth, it would make everything easier. But, we don't have that capability."

Nova raised her brows. "Finding a way to contact Earth or the Earth Colony Alliance might be an easier goal than taking over a ship."

"The message would take years to get there and who knows if the ECA would even send a rescue ship to such a distant colony." Taryn shook her head. "I can't rely on chance alone. I'll send a message from the alien ship, but I also want the technology to save us in the near future, too. I much prefer being in control."

Nova snorted. "Sometimes a little too much in control, in my opinion."

"A leader letting loose doesn't exactly instill confidence," she drawled.

"Then promise me that once you save the planet, you let me show you some fun. No one should die before riding the sloping Veran waterfalls."

Taryn sighed and sank into the chair in front of Nova's desk. "Fine. But how about we focus on capturing the aliens first?"

Nova removed a sheaf of crude paper made from the purple wood of the local trees and took out an ink pot and golden feather. "I'll come up with a fool-proof capture plan, but I hope you keep me in the loop about what happens next."

"I will when it's time. I need to see who we're dealing with before making concrete plans."

Dipping her feather into the ink pot, Nova scratched a few notes on the purple paper. "Then let me get to work. The staging is mostly done already, but I need to think beyond that. Since we've never tried to capture a large ship before, it's going to take some time. I think someone captured a shuttle in the past, but we'll see if I can find the record."

"You always go on about how you love challenges."

"Don't remind me." She made a shooing motion toward the door. "And this is one of the few times I can tell my settlement leader to get lost and let me work."

Taryn stood. "If you need me, I'll be in the outside garden."

"Fine, fine. Just go. You're making it hard to concentrate." Nova looked up with a smile. "And you're also delaying my next project."

"Do I want to know?"

"It's called Operation Fun Times." Nova pointed her quill. "I sense you're going to land an alien this time. You're a talented individual, except when it comes to flirting. I'm going to help with that."

Shaking her head, Taryn muttered, "Have fun," and left her old-time friend to her own devices. Maybe someday Nova would understand that while Taryn missed the antics of their youth, she enjoyed taking care of her people more.

Still, she'd admit that it would be nice to finally have the chance to get a man of her own. Most of her family was gone, and like many of the women of her age group, Taryn would love the option to start one.

Not now, Demara. You won't have a chance unless you succeed in capturing the visitors.

With the play planning in motion, Taryn had one more important task to set up before she could also pore through the records and look for ideas.

As much as she wished for everything to go smoothly, it could take a turn and end up horribly wrong. In that case, she needed an out. Namely, she needed to erase memories. The trick would be conferring with her head medicine woman to find the balance between erasing memories and rendering the aliens brain-dead. As the early Jasvarians had discovered, the forgetful plant was both a blessing and a curse. Without it, they'd never have survived this long. However, in the wrong dose, it could turn someone into a vegetable and ruin their chances.

Don't worry. Matilda knows what she's doing. Picking up her pace, Taryn exited the mountain into the late-day sun. The faint purple and blue hues of the mountains and trees were an everyday sight to her, but she still found the colors beautiful. Her great-grandmother's tales had been full of green leaves and blue skies back on Earth. A part of Taryn wanted to see another world, but the leader in her would never abandon the people of Jasvar.

Looking to the pinkish sky, she only hoped the visitors fell for her tricks. Otherwise, Taryn might have to admit defeat and prepare her people for the worst.

The Conquest is now available in paperback.

Persuading the Dragon

STONEFIRE DRAGONS #12

Nearly a year ago, a human female showed up on Stone-fire's land carrying a flash drive full of information stolen from the Dragon Knights. However, before Zain Kinsella could interrogate her, she soon fell into a coma and hasn't awoken since. His initial anger fades and he starts to wonder if the thin, pale girl would ever wake again. When she does, it's up to him to help guard her and make her strong enough to face some questioning. He most definitely shouldn't notice her delicious heat or the sadness in her eyes. She's their prisoner, and can be nothing more.

Ivy Passmore finds herself inside a dragon-shifter's hospital, bedridden and barely able to sit up. Despite the over-whelming grief at the death of her brother, she's determined to do everything she can to atone for her part in helping the Dragon Knights and causing her brother's murder. She's more than ready to tell the dragons everything. Soon one tall, quiet Protector makes a deal—she endures his physical therapy and he'll help track down her brother's killers. Ivy has no choice but to agree and slowly her idea of dragon-shifters changes, especially around one certain dragonman.

As two former enemies morph into something more, the Department of Dragon Affairs finds out about Ivy and demands she be surrendered. Will Zain do his duty and hand her over? Or, will they be able to find a way to be together?

———————————

Persuading the Dragon will be available in paperback in late May 2020.

The Dragon's Choice

TAHOE DRAGON MATES #1

After Jose Santos's younger sister secretly enters them both into the yearly dragon lottery and they get selected, he begrudgingly agrees to participate. It means picking a human female from a giant room full of them and staying around just long enough to get her pregnant. However, when his dragon notices one female who keeps hiding behind a book, Jose has a new plan—win his fated mate, no matter what it takes.

Victoria Lewis prefers being home with a book and away from large crowds. But she desperately wants to study dragon-shifters at close range, so she musters up her courage to enter the dragon lottery. When she's selected as one of the potential candidates, she decides to accept her spot. After all, it's not as if the dragon-shifter will pick her—an introverted bookworm who prefers jeans and sweats to skirts or fancy clothes. Well, until he's standing right in front of her with flashing eyes and says he wants her.

As Jose tries to win his fated female, trouble stirs inside his clan. Will he be able to keep his mate with him forever? Or will the American Department of Dragon Affairs whisk her away to some other clan to protect her?

NOTE: This is a quick, steamy standalone story about fated mates and sexy dragon-shifters near Lake Tahoe in the USA. You don't have to read all my other dragon books to enjoy this one!

The Dragon's Choice will be available in paperback in early March 2020.

Also by Jessie Donovan

Asylums for Magical Threats

Blaze of Secrets (AMT #1)

Frozen Desires (AMT #2)

Shadow of Temptation (AMT #3)

Flare of Promise (AMT #4)

Cascade Shifters

Convincing the Cougar (CS #0.5)

Reclaiming the Wolf (CS #1)

Cougar's First Christmas (CS #2)

Resisting the Cougar (CS #3)

Kelderan Runic Warriors

The Conquest (KRW #1)

The Barren (KRW #2)

The Heir (KRW #3)

The Forbidden (KRW #4)

The Hidden (KRW #5)

The Survivor / Kajala Mayven (KRW #6 / 2020)

Lochguard Highland Dragons

The Dragon's Dilemma (LHD #1)

The Dragon Guardian (LHD #2)

The Dragon's Heart (LHD #3)

The Dragon Warrior (LHD #4)

The Dragon Family (LHD #5)

The Dragon's Discovery (LHD #6)

The Dragon's Pursuit (LHD #7)

The Dragon Collective / Cat & Lachlan (LHD #8 / TBD)

Love in Scotland

Crazy Scottish Love (LiS #1)

Chaotic Scottish Wedding (LiS #2)

Stonefire Dragons

Sacrificed to the Dragon (SD #1)

Seducing the Dragon (SD #2)

Revealing the Dragons (SD #3)

Healed by the Dragon (SD #4)

Reawakening the Dragon (SD #5)

Loved by the Dragon (SD #6)

Surrendering to the Dragon (SD #7)

Cured by the Dragon (SD #8)

Aiding the Dragon (SD #9)

Finding the Dragon (SD #10)

Craved by the Dragon (SD #11)

Persuading the Dragon / Zain and Ivy (SD #12 / May 14, 2020)

Stonefire Dragons Shorts

Meeting the Humans (SDS #1)

The Dragon Camp (SDS #2)

The Dragon Play (SDS #3)

Stonefire Dragons Universe

Winning Skyhunter (SDU #1)

Transforming Snowridge (SDU #2)

Tahoe Dragon Mates

The Dragon's Choice (TDM #1 / Feb 27, 2020)

The Dragon's Need (TDM #2 / March 26, 2020)

The Dragon's Bidder (TDM #3 / Summer 2020)

About the Author

Jessie Donovan has sold over half a million books, has given away hundreds of thousands more to readers for free, and has even hit the *NY Times* and *USA Today* bestseller lists. She is best known for her dragon-shifter series, but also writes about magic users, aliens, and even has a crazy romantic comedy series set in Scotland. When not reading a book, attempting to tame her yard, or traipsing around some foreign country on a shoestring, she can often be found interacting with her readers on Facebook. She lives near Seattle, where, yes, it rains a lot but it also makes everything green.

Visit her website at: www.JessieDonovan.com

Made in the USA
Coppell, TX
02 December 2020

42689866R00163